The Magic of
Airy Poodini

The Magic of Airy Poodini

John's Fart-Ripping Adventures Book 2

John Pahrsink

Derelict Books

To the late President Gerald Ford: *Politics aside, I applaud you for blaming all the farts during your presidency on your secret service detail.*

FOREWORD
A RECAP FROM THE JOHN

I see you made the novel decision of picking up my second... novel. Brilliant! Do you remember what happened in my last story? (I know publishing these things takes a while.)

The story started on my first day at a new school. I made some new friends and... That's where the clichés stopped because the next thing I knew, I was farting ghosts. Does any of this sound familiar?

I hope so. But maybe you're reading these books out of order. That's kind of weird, but I fart ghosts, so who am I to judge?

Either way, here's a recap of our story thus far:

My name is John Pahrsink the second. At the end of summer, my family (Mom, Dad, my sister Leyla, and I) moved from boring old Iowa to the only slightly less boring suburbs of Chicago.

The first day of fifth grade started with a trip to the museum. It ended with a curse.

An accident that was totally not my fault resulted in an ancient Egyptian vase falling off a display pedestal. There was a wheel of cheese inside that got mixed up with my lunch.

After taking a bite of that cheese, King Tut started showing up along with my farts. Well, some of them anyway.

In the following days, I thought I had the curse all figured out. My fart ghost—King Toot, as I liked to call him—only shows up with the worst farts. You know, the real stinkers.

The historical king promised he'd lift the curse. But there was a catch. I had to return his belongings. And by 'belongings,' I mean every single artifact removed from his tomb.

Oh.

There's one other issue with my 'situation'.

It's not just King Toot.

I'm capable of farting out other ghosts too. And with that, we'll pick up where the first book left off.

CHAPTER 1
QUAKE-ERING IN MY PANTS

The ghosts of King Tut and Larry the Quaker Oats guy walked into my bedroom. It sounds like the start of a bad joke, but it's not. Or if it is, it's not a funny one seeing as how they floated out of my butt. Rude.

The transparent Egyptian ruler hovered circles around the curly-haired old man. Toot seemed just as confused as me about his sudden appearance.

I knew precisely two things about this new ghostly "companion." First, his name was Larry—he'd introduced himself moments ago. Second, his wide-brimmed hat and high-collar shirt with the white scarf thingy matched the dude on the granola bar wrapper.

Larry's black eyes focused on the spinning ceiling fan and back at me.

"Where the dickens am I?"

His voice was deeper than King Toot's, but he was an old man, not a teen. It also held that cranky tone that old people sometimes get.

It made a certain sort of sense. When I first farted out King Toot, he was confused and babbling ancient Egyptian, which I couldn't understand.

Plus, Larry had already asked once where he was and probably thought I'd been ignoring him. For the record, I wasn't. Farting out two ghosts at once takes a lot out of a kid.

He floated directly at me, passing through a cardboard box I still hadn't unpacked. His head jerked around with a sense of urgency, inspecting the rest of his surroundings while he advanced.

"Where. Am. I?"

"Shhh..." I said, before really thinking.

It wouldn't have mattered if he'd let out a blood-curdling scream. I was the only one who could hear the ghosts, except for my friends who'd gotten a whiff of the cursed cheese.

Larry ignored me and kept coming.

My stomach lurched like that time Dad ran over a tortoise on the highway.

I couldn't let him touch me.

Sorry, this is an important bit I didn't mention for the first-time readers. Larry may have seemed harmless, but I never elaborated on my *first* ghostly encounter. Toot's touch transported my consciousness thousands of years into the past. To ancient Egypt, to be precise.

While there, I felt every bit of the heat from the flames burning inside Tut's palace. Something told me the curse operated under horror movie rules:

Dying in one of these ghostly realms meant game over in real life.

I knew nothing about the Quaker Oats guy.

If he touched me, I could end up in the past, confused for a witch, and burnt at the stake.

I somersaulted over my bed and grabbed the knob of my bedroom door.

King Toot held his ground.

"WHERE AM..."

Before Larry reached me, I swung open the door as fast as possible. The fart particles forming Larry's old, wrinkled face scattered to the wind.

Toot rested his ghostly hands on his hips (or the tapered section where they would have been) and grinned.

He knew this drill. I'd done the same thing to him. And my buddy had also spritzed him with air freshener.

"Uhh," I said. "This is awkward."

The Pharaoh's ghost snorted and kept his distance.

"Truce?" I said, letting go of the doorknob and holding my hands up in surrender.

When Toot didn't charge me, I took that as a 'yes.'

"So is Larry... one of yours?"

"Never met him in my life," he said.

"But he's part of the..." I swallowed. "Curse?"

He shrugged.

What? How could he not know?

The silver wrapper on my bed caught my attention. That granola bar was the last thing I'd eaten. Obviously, I didn't understand the curse as well as previously thought.

Was Larry a punishment for trying to trick my way out of the arrangement I'd made? Could Toot read my mind?

CAN YOU? I thought as loud as possible in my head. *CAN YOU READ MY MIND?*

I stared right through his very soul and projected the thoughts again.

Toot's gaseous form bobbed up and down as usual but showed no reaction.

You can't hear me at all, can you?

No, of course he couldn't. He was a fart ghost, not a psychic. While that was a good thing, it didn't offset the fact that I had a second spirit haunting me.

"We still have a deal, right? You'll break the curse after I return your things?"

"Indeed," the ghost said. "If you keep up your end of the bargain, we will lift the curse."

"Wait. We?"

Honestly, I wasn't surprised at this point. Why not add a few more unanswered questions to the giant pile?

Did *we* mean my fart ghost and me? Or did it mean him and Larry?

That led to even more important questions.

How long would two ghosts fly out of my butt? And how many ghosts could I manage at once?

When I looked up, I caught the literal tail end of Toot passing through my bedroom wall. I ran to the window and watched his form slip into the darkness.

Apparently, he had things to do besides torment me.

So did I: learning how an oatmeal mascot tied into an ancient Egyptian curse. Hopefully, the internet had answers.

Unfortunately, I had no way to access the internet at the moment. Mom and Dad felt I wasn't old enough for a phone, and Leyla never let me borrow hers. I glanced at the alarm clock. It was nearly ten p.m., already past my bedtime.

I'd sneaked downstairs plenty of times, but I couldn't do it right in front of my parents. They were in the den watching television... on the couch five feet from the family computer.

Luckily, my new school was fancy. Every student got their own laptop to take home.

This is where Mom's organizational obsession paid off. Every day after school, she made my sister and me leave our bags on the bench beside the stairs. I could reach over the railing without ever setting foot downstairs. It was the perfect heist. Unless Dad's sweet tooth took over and led him to the pantry at the wrong time.

But it would only take me a minute. Tops.

I popped my head into the hallway. A line of light shone beneath Leyla's door, accompanied by faint music. It was a great sign. She should have been asleep, too, which meant she couldn't rat me out.

The railing was smooth against my palm as I crept down the stairs. One step. Two. Three. Almost there.

I froze as the house shook. Either a T-Rex had started a rampage or Dad needed snacks.

I hugged the wall and hoped against the third option. If Dad headed for his private pooping palace (his name for the master bathroom), he'd run into me.

"Bring me back a bottle of water," Mom called from the distance.

"Got it."

Dad sounded right next to me, but I'm sure it was my imagination.

The microwave beeped. A cabinet thudded shut and ice cubes clinked against a glass.

As Dad's heavy footfalls headed away, I took my chance.

I leaned over the railing, thrust my hand into the open backpack, and seized the computer... Just as the first of a dozen gunshots echoed through the hallway.

CHAPTER 2
ADVERTISEMENTS AND YOGA FARTS

Okay. Obviously, nobody shot up my house. But you know how it is. When you're doing something you shouldn't, your ears are on full alert. A popcorn kernel might sound like an explosion. Or in my case, a gunshot.

It's a good thing I'd already farted, because this would have scared another ghost out of me. My heart pounded and a falling sensation took over as I tottered down the stairs.

My arms flailed as the banister dug into my stomach. I stretched as far as possible and braced one foot against the wall. Somehow, my free hand grabbed one of the poles and kept me from going headfirst onto the entryway tile.

I regained my footing in time for my backpack to fall forward. Naturally, the popcorn took a break from doing its thing and the loud thunk rang out through the house.

"What was that?" Mom said, muffled by the sound of popcorn picking back up again.

"Probably one of the kids." Dad sighed. "I'll go check."

I hurried up the stairs, praying the popcorn would cover my retreat.

I flipped the light switch, pushed the door closed—though not far enough that the lock clicked—and stashed the laptop beneath my pillow.

Hopefully, Dad didn't notice the laptop missing from the backpack.

One one-thousand, two one-thousand, I counted in my head. How long would walking through the house take? I'd never paced it out before. Though, now I'd found a reason.

Eight one-thousand, nine...

When I eventually lost track, I flipped open the laptop.

A quick internet search gave me the answer I'd been looking for.

Well, sort of.

My new fart ghost was one hundred percent the Quaker oatmeal guy. But he wasn't a real person. 'Larry' was a fictional character based off William Penn, the founder of the province of Pennsylvania. As in one of the original thirteen colonies.

I read on.

For your sake, I'll summarize the boring company history. The Quaker Oats Company formed not long after America declared their independence from Britain. Their Quaker man mascot "Larry" didn't come around until a hundred years later.

I did some more fact checking.

William Penn died long before anyone discovered King Tut's tomb. Which meant Larry and Penn shouldn't have had any ties to the curse.

My eyes lost focus on the screen as I wrestled with that newfound information.

Larry was an advertisement. I farted him because of the curse. Eliminating cheese from my diet wouldn't help.

My lips quivered.

What about breakfast cereal? Would leprechauns or giant rabbits come out of my butt? A starving, sugar-fueled tiger would *not* be Grrreat.

A shiver ran down my spine as the full implications struck me. Why would the curse stop with cereal?

A disembodied head with a mustache. A huge smiling glass pitcher who loved crashing through walls. Tree-dwelling elves. Not to mention giant red bears who loved wiping their butts.

Granted, I've never eaten toilet paper, but you get my point.

Like Larry, they were all figments of some marketing professional's twisted imagination.

Forget becoming dinner, if an imaginary animal touched me, I'd become imaginary too. Or worse, stuck in some executive's head.

I took a series of deep breaths to (unsuccessfully) calm myself.

Earlier investigation told me that food can stay in your digestive tract for up to eight hours before... coming out the other end.

King Toot was an exception. I'd never fully pass him until I—well, *he*—broke the curse.

More questions filled my head.

Was the Quaker Oatmeal guy with me for another seven hours or an eternity?

Toot wanted back all the treasures stolen from him. Completely understandable. Who knew what a fake ghost based on the founder of Pennsylvania wanted?

And what the heck was a Quaker anyway?

I pulled the laptop closer and pecked at the keys.

What is a Quaker?

An individual belonging to the Religious Society of Friends. Collectively, they believe in spreading peace, equality, and following one's 'inner light.'

My heart slowed and my breathing evened out.

A lifelong curse for accidentally eating some cheese was the farthest thing from peace and equality. Could I convince Larry to negotiate a better arrangement on my behalf?

You know, fight fire with fire. Or farts with farts, in this case.

I sighed.

This would have been helpful information *before* slamming a door through him. At least Quakers were against violence. Larry would have to forgive me. Right?

But I had to deal with one problem at a time. First, I had to bring him back.

I sucked in a deep breath and pushed until my face went red. Of course the one time I wanted to fart, nothing happened. As I shifted on the bed, the granola bar wrapper crinkled beneath me.

Maybe I needed more granola bars.

I hopped out of bed, using the laptop's glow to guide my way to the light switch.

Music still came from beneath my sister's closed door. All good on that front. But could I get to the pantry?

I had to. This was important.

I snuck down the stairs all ninja-like and peeked around the corner.

Mom and Dad sat cuddled together on the couch, bathed in the television's blue glow. While I couldn't make out what they were watching, it must not have held Dad's attention. His chainsaw-like snores drowned out the audio entirely.

I stayed low, crawling to the pantry Dad had conveniently left open. This is where I got especially lucky. The granola bars were on the floor right in front of me. Mom always complained how the giant box wouldn't fit on the shelf but kept buying them.

After grabbing a handful of bars, I retreated to my room just as stealthily.

I closed the door and dumped my bounty on the bed. As if the curse wasn't bad enough, they were all my least favorite flavors: three peanut butter and two dried-up grape turd (raisin, for the uneducated).

But the curse had to go, so I unwrapped each one and mashed them together. I took the single mega bar, shoved it in my mouth, and chewed.

And chewed.

And chewed until my jaw ached.

It was about then that I realized my mistake. Five lumps of scratchy oats do a number on your throat. Unfortunately, as soon as I went near the door I heard the bottom stair creak.

Getting water would have to wait.

I flipped the switch and crept back to the bed, shutting the laptop. Like earlier, the dark enhanced my hearing.

There was a click of a door opening, followed by Mom scolding Leyla for still being awake. The door across the hall clicked again.

I rolled on top of the computer just as my door cracked. Mom's presence lingered like an unwanted fart.

My nose whistled as I breathed heavily. I still hadn't choked down my snack and I knew I was toast. Any second now, she'd bust me using that special sense all mom's possess.

However, Mom wasn't on her A-game that night. She bought my fake snores *and* missed the pile of wrappers on the bed.

The door clicked again, plunging the room into darkness.

By then, my mouth was full of saliva, giving me what I needed to swallow the unholy union of peanut butter and raisin.

Her bedroom door echoed through the hallway, and I finally had time to think.

I'd had this curse for three days now. Even though tooting King Toot had been permanently etched into my memory, I couldn't recall how soon my troubles began after eating his cursed cheese.

Best guess? Forty-five minutes.

I'd been paying attention to the clock this time. Larry had shown up fifteen minutes after my granola bar snack.

"Guess I should start a journal of each meal and the resulting farts," I said aloud with a sigh.

The farts held the key, and I'd done extensive research about which foods caused gas. Granola and oats weren't specifically on that list, but they contained loads of fiber.

Everyone knew fiber made you poop. And what were farts but a trumpet announcing a turd's arrival?

I clutched my stomach. I'd just consumed a ton of fiber, but I didn't feel anything yet. Unfortunately—or maybe fortunately—digestion occurred slowly.

I went back to the laptop. If the internet knew about Larry, it could probably help speed things along down there, too.

How to fart.

Results filled the screen.

How to fart... *without creating any sound.* I should have bookmarked that one, but it wasn't what I needed at that moment.

How to fart... *directly into the microphone.* Uhh... What?

How to fart: *Yoga poses to naturally relieve gas and bloating.*

Bingo!

A GIF of a blonde woman with a huge rear end demonstrated something called 'happy baby pose.' I scrolled down and found several more. Child's pose. The seated forward bend.

The list went on and on, ending with...

Wind-relieving pose.

Yoga had nothing to do with exercising. It was just a farting club for moms. Who knew?

I paid close attention to the instructional video. It seemed simple enough. You lie on your back, tuck your knees to your chest, and rock back and forth while holding them.

"Here goes nothing," I mumbled.

I hugged my knees and rocked side to side. After a minute or so, there was no noticeable change in my stomach. The website didn't exactly say how long this would take.

I swayed faster, hoping it would speed things up. All it did was inch me closer to the edge of the bed.

There was a brief second of free-fall before I hit the floor. My knees forced the air from my lungs. I rolled onto my back and took a grasping breath as the light in my room switched on.

I squinted, lifted my head, and found Dad standing over me.

"Are you o—"

His voice trailed off as he took in the woman doing yoga on my laptop. And the pile of granola bar wrappers.

"You know Mom doesn't want you eating up here. Or using screens an hour prior to bedtime." He glanced at the clock on my nightstand. "Which was over an hour ago."

"But you and Mom watch TV every night just before bed," is what I *wanted* to say. Given the circumstances, I knew better.

"I lost track of time while looking up stretches."

He picked up the laptop and hit a few keys.

"And if you want to get rid of gas, try eating more dinner and less junk food."

If only it were that easy.

I crumpled the wrappers into a ball. "Sorry."

"I'll put this back in your bag." He closed the lid and reminded me to brush my teeth before leaving the room.

Phew.

No punishment. And, more importantly, no awkward conversations about the yoga lady's butt.

This was a clear sign from the universe to try again tomorrow. I cleaned up the wrappers, brushed my teeth, got a sip of water from the sink, and called it a night. We'd already established that I fart in my sleep. Maybe things would work itself out.

And that was the end of the chapter.

Or so I thought.

"Get back in your room, Leyla!"

My dad's voice jolted me awake. I blinked the sleep from my eyes and checked the clock. Just after three in the morning.

I slid out of bed with a yawn and stuck my head into the dark hallway.

Dad crept down the stairs with a baseball bat in hand.

Mom and Leyla's heads peeked out from their rooms like me.

"What's going on?" I asked, rubbing my eyes.

"Get back in your rooms," Mom whispered.

"Someone rang the doorbell," said Leyla, ignoring her. "Probably the escaped ax murderer from down the street."

Mom whispered something, but was drowned out by the front door rattling under the heavy fist of something desperately wanting in.

CHAPTER 3
CURSED AND JINXED

Was it Toot returning from his mystery trip?

The Quaker ghost?

An undiscovered ghost farted out while I slept?

Nope. That was silly. Ghosts didn't knock.

I glanced at Leyla. Neither did ax murderers.

You know who did?

Cops. And museum curators. And angry museum cops hunting children who ruined their precious display pieces.

"Get back in your rooms," Mom demanded again as Dad readied the bat.

I backed up a step and closed the door until only a crack remained. She couldn't see me, but I still had a straight shot down the stairs. I had to know who was at the door.

Dad checked the peep hole and sighed. He leaned the bat against the wall before turning on the light and unlocking the door.

"Sorry..." Dad said. "We weren't expecting you."

Presuming it was safe, I stepped up to the railing.

Leyla pushed in close to me. "Who is it?"

I shrugged. Dad took his sweet time moving out of the way.

"No idea," I said as Dad grabbed a large duffle bag from the woman who stepped into the house. Her curly hair stuck out at all angles as if she licked electrical outlets for fun. A tie-dyed linen skirt fell just short of a pair of faded combat boots.

I recognized my aunt's crazy fashion sense without seeing the patch-covered leather jacket.

"Johnathan," she said.

Aunt Lucille was the only one who called dad by his full name. It drove him nuts.

Dad glanced up at Mom with a look she usually reserved after one of us did something dumb. She looked equally stunned.

Me on the other hand? I knew exactly why Aunt Lucille was here. She'd called last night with one of her psychic premonitions.

Looking down at her, I could clearly hear her voice ringing in my ears.

John, you're in grave danger.

Aunt Lucille was a true believer. Otherwise, she wouldn't have driven five hours from Kentucky.

"Aunt Lucy!" Leyla yelled. She took the stairs two at a time and held her arms out.

Our usually touchy-feely aunt dodged my sister with a graceful twirl. Leyla gave her an awkward embrace from behind.

Aunt Lucille broke free from my sister's bony arms and in one smooth motion whipped around, revealing a sleeping kitten inside her jacket.

"Be careful," Aunt Lucille said, holding the animal aloft. "You'll crush John's spirit guide."

The tiny black pile of fur stretched and let out a yawn before curling back up.

"Uhh..." was all I could get out.

"Excuse me?" Dad said.

Leyla wrestled the kitten out of my aunt's hands and cradled it against her chest. "Can we keep her?"

"Jinx," our aunt said with a smile.

"Please, Mom? I'll change its litter every day and feed it and take care of it."

"John?" Mom asked.

Dad's jaw moved, but no words came out.

Mom sighed the way she always did when Dad forced the important decisions on her.

"We'll talk about this in the morning."

Seriously? I thought. *They're going to let us keep that flea bag?*

We'd never had a family pet before. Aside from goldfish from the state fair which never lived longer than a couple of weeks. Leyla had never expressed any interest in owning a cat before. And me? I considered myself a dog person.

"Why are you here?" Dad asked.

Mom glared at him, though he wasn't looking. "John!"

"What I meant to say is, it's the middle of the night and we weren't expecting you." He glanced back at Mom, who shook her head.

None of it phased Aunt Lucille. "It was of the utmost importance that I came."

I gulped.

While I'd mentioned the curse on the phone, I hadn't gone into detail. Aunt Lucille was well known for dominating every conversation. But I told her to keep it a secret from my parents. I think...

"Brand new homes must be treated with respect, otherwise you can get off on the wrong foot." She looked up at me and winked.

Neither Mom nor Dad explained that we'd been in the house for the better part of three months. They just sort of accepted it as part of her general kookiness. Or at the very least, neither of them had the heart to turn her away.

Dad slapped his thighs. "Well, we don't have a spare bedroom, but we can set up the inflatable bed for you in the den. Unless you'd prefer sleeping under the stars."

I caught another of Mom's glares from the corner of my eye that Dad missed.

"Thank you," Aunt Lucille said. "An air mattress would be perfect."

Dad trudged up the stairs. "At least she kept her other thirty-eight cats at home," he whispered as he passed Mom.

She didn't smile, but he winked at me when I did.

"Leyla, please grab a set of sheets for your aunt's bed," Mom said.

"I'll do it!" I grabbed a set from the linen closet next to my room and tucked them under my arm. When Dad came back, I took the heavy inflatable bed from him.

Leyla nuzzled Jinx against her cheek and closed her bedroom door behind her.

I headed down the stairway while Mom and Dad processed everything (and before they could start asking questions).

"Back in bed as soon as your aunt gets situated," Mom said.

"And the laptop stays downstairs," Dad added.

"Okay."

I didn't need the laptop anymore. Not when my "expert on everything psychic and spooky" aunt was here.

Whack.

Each hurried step down the stairs slammed the heavy plastic pump into my leg.

"Ow," I muttered.

Whack.

I slowed my pace to save a few bruises. The curse had been in place for several days, what was another few minutes?

I dragged the bag into the family room, dumped it out, and got to work. The vacuum pump whirred as I held down the button. My eyes lost focus as my thoughts fought against the annoying sound.

You were right Aunt Lucille. I am in danger. I'm enslaved by my farts.

Nope. She wouldn't take me seriously if I said it like that. Even if it was the simplest explanation. Thoughts swirled in my head. None of them were great. I needed a way to put things into her language.

I dropped the pump and jumped as thick spider webbing fell in front of my eyes. I swatted the strands away before realizing they were twine.

"Don't mind me," Aunt Lucille said, pulling on the line she'd looped over the ceiling fan.

I traced the string upward to the suspended dreamcatcher. Maybe I needed one of those.

Aunt Lucille dusted her hands off and planted them on her hips. "Tell me everything."

"Umm..." I glanced at the button for the air bed but doubted it would buy me any more time.

"I can't help you if you don't tell me what happened."

"King Tut is haunting me because I stole from him!"

I feared the worst as the words spewed from my mouth, but my aunt didn't flinch.

She slumped down on her knees. For a second, I thought I had killed her, but she hit the floor and furiously searched her bags.

"No," muttered Aunt Lucille. "No. No. No. I didn't bring anything suitable for tackling a mummy."

She hopped back up, grabbed my shoulders, and turned me this way and that.

"At least the rot hasn't taken hold yet."

My eyes grew as big as dinner plates. "The what?"

"Mummy rot," she said. "I'm glad I came when I did."

"King Tut isn't a mummy. He's a ghost."

Aunt Lucille blinked. "Egyptian funeral rites always include mummification. It can't be a ghost. Now, tell me how you found yourself wrapped up in mummy business."

I sighed. "My class went to a museum, and I knocked into an old vase that belonged to King Tut. There was a wheel of cheese inside and it ended up in my lunch."

I paused, watching for an eye roll, a raised eyebrow, anything that'd tell me she thought I'd been messing with her.

She sat patiently, waiting for me to go on.

"After taking a bite of it, I got ill. That's when King Toot appeared."

"King... Toot?"

My mouth clamped shut. There it was. A faint curl of her lip. I'd blown it.

"His ghost only shows up when I... uhh... pass gas."

Aunt Lucille turned away from me and muttered something I couldn't make out.

I tugged on her sleeve. "I'm not poking fun at you. I'm serious."

My aunt let out an exhausted sigh and flopped backward. Her bare legs rubbed against the air mattress, letting out a loud rubbery fart. Kinda funny but it didn't help my cause one bit.

I tried the puppy dog eye trick on her, but she'd shut her eyes... Eyes lined by dark circles.

Who could blame her? From her perspective, she'd driven all night for me to crack fart jokes.

There was nothing left to do but continue my story.

"Until I return all of King Tut's stolen artifacts, I'm stuck serving as his Ushabti. And now there are other ghosts harassing me too."

She finally met my eyes again. "What?"

"Some guy named Larry," I said, scratching an itch on my nose. "Who may or may not have founded the colony of Pennsylvania."

Aunt Lucille shook her head. "No. What was that other word you said."

"Ushabti. It means—"

"Answerer," said Aunt Lucille. She stared off into the distance for a moment. "So, this isn't just a fart joke?"

"I wish it was."

"Okay," she said, returning to her bag. "Spirits, I can manage."

She piled things onto the coffee table.

Baggies full of leaves. A container of salt. Red and white candles.

"John," Dad's voice carried down from above. "Bedtime!"

I knew that tone—the one before Dad started taking away my screen privileges.

"I'm coming," I yelled back.

Aunt Lucille grabbed my wrist and held me back.

"Will you survive until the morning?"

As much as I wanted the curse gone, another day wouldn't kill me. My fart ghosts weren't going anywhere.

"Uh huh," I said with a nod.

I don't remember trudging upstairs or falling asleep. Which is odd because I remember the part where I stubbed my toe on a heavy moving box. But I did remember an intense flash of heat across my face and protecting my eyes with my hand.

When I lowered them, I found the flaming braziers of King Tut's grand palace in place of my bed. Massive sandstone bricks in place of my walls.

Crap.

I should have told my aunt that Tut occasionally abducts me.

CHAPTER 4
HONEY GOAT CHERI-WOES

Someone cleared their throat.

I spun around and found myself staring at King Tut atop his elaborate golden throne. The actual flesh-and-bone King Tut, not the transparent ghostly version. They looked similar, of course, but my last visit to Egypt had left me feeling that King Tutankhamun and King Toot were separate entities somehow.

Though, I still hadn't been able to prove or disprove that theory. Or figure out whether that worked in my favor.

"Ushabti," his voice boomed. "Your first tribute..."

I held my breath.

"Is acceptable." He made a sweeping gesture and gave the shallowest of nods.

Phew.

"I'm glad you enjoyed it," I said. Or at least, I *tried* to say. My ears didn't understand the words coming from my lips even though I knew what they meant.

I fought a sudden urge to yell out potty words just to figure out what they sounded like in his strange, dead language. However, the museum doctor's mention of a fart causing a bloody rebellion in ancient Egypt kept me in check.

That's when I noticed a table I hadn't seen during my prior visit. My eyes scanned the room looking for other things out of place.

Tut lifted his chin, watching me closely, and leaned back against his throne. It seemed I had his permission to refamiliarize myself with my surroundings.

It was like I remembered.

The palace was spacious, at least a couple of stories tall, supported by grand columns covered in hieroglyphics. Large metal baskets held roaring piles of burning firewood.

I wasn't exactly in a dream. Those flames were hot. (I'd learned that the hard way last time).

The other important thing to note is that I couldn't leave. And not just because Tut wouldn't allow me. There were literally no windows, doors, or other discernible escape routes.

The stone table against the wall was the only new addition. It wasn't your typical kitchen table designed to seat a family of six. This thing was meant for banquets. With intricate maze-like carvings along the side and a red, woven runner accented with gold, the table was fit for royalty (because, you know, he was).

As gigantic as the table was, it only held a single item: a small, golden pot. Its lid lay slightly ajar, leaving room for the handle of a jewel-encrusted spoon. Whatever that container held let off a faint glow impossible to resist.

My captor watched patiently as my feet carried me over to the table. I got on my tiptoes and peered inside. Thousands of thin red hairs overlapped one another.

But it wasn't a jar of red panda hair. That was my first offering to King Tut.

Saffron, courtesy of my friend Akira.

As I looked up and down at the length of the table, a light bulb went off in my head. The table was there for my offerings. Filling this thing would take me forever.

So much for hoping the most expensive spice in existence would get me out of this mess.

I turned in place, and my stomach dropped.

Except for that table, the columns, and the fire pits, the pyramid was one big empty space. A pyramid bigger than four school gyms slapped together.

It wouldn't take me hundreds or thousands of offerings. It would take a lifetime.

My hands trembled.

One lifetime wouldn't be enough. I'd be stuck farting ghosts until I died.

That was if he'd *let* me die. This was a curse after all.

I shook my head. That was silly. Of course I could die. Cursed cheese wasn't a secret source of immortality. But once I died, I'd probably end up as a ghost myself, stuck serving Tutankhamun for all eternity.

Or worse. Haunting his next victim's rear end.

"Get a grip, John," I mumbled in ancient Egyptian. The more time wasted here meant less time solving the curse.

The only problem was I didn't know how to get home. Last time, someone on the outside pulled me back.

King Tut sat on his throne in silence, content to watch me squirm.

I looked up to the top of the pyramid, bathed in pitch black, hoping my aunt was up there somewhere.

What are you waiting for, Aunt Lucille? Get me out!

My silent cry for help went nowhere. Either she was asleep already, or Tut held some kind of magic blocking her from hearing me.

There was third option, of course. That my aunt wasn't psychic at all. But I didn't like entertaining that one.

I lowered my head and inched my way back toward King Tut, giving myself time to think.

Did he want something else from me?

I pulled my pockets inside out. Unless he wanted a penny, some lint, and a little "inspected by #37" sticker from the pants factory, I had nothing of value.

Should I offer him something from home?

A box of mac and cheese? A can of Dr. Pepper? Goldfish crackers? Nobody would notice them missing from our pantry.

But that was all processed food he'd know nothing about.

Beef jerky?

I shook my head and thought about what my aunt had said. Funeral rites in Egypt included mummification.

And what were mummies but human beef jerky?

What do we have at home that the ancient Egyptians would have eaten?

Tea had been around forever. They probably drank some sort of tea and Mom had boxes of the stuff.

No. King Tut was eighteen years old when he died. He was just a kid. And what kind of kid likes tea?

It had to be something sweet. But they didn't have processed sugar back then so Oreos or Hostess cupcakes wouldn't cut it either. All that sugar would make him vomit.

Wait. Vomit is exactly what I needed.

But not any old vomit. Bee vomit!

Honey was sweet and they must have had it in ancient times. But did bees live in the desert?

Tut must have seen the cogs turning in my head because he leaned forward.

Here goes nothing.

"Uhh..." My voice cracked. "Mr. Tutankhamun, sir."

Sir? Ugh. Even in a foreign language, it sounded cringy.

I coughed into my fist and tried again.

"If you let me leave, I promise I'll return with a jar of the finest honey."

Tutankhamun's eyes narrowed.

I straightened my back and prepared to dive away from the lasers that would surely come out of his eyes.

"Honey is a wise tribute."

It is?

He nodded, noticing the surprise on my face.

"Despite our differences, you understand that bees were sacred creatures and their honey even more so."

"They are?" That time I failed to keep the words in my head.

"I had dozens of royal beekeepers who raised colonies in pots made from Nile River clay. Honey is an important symbol of resurrection and wards off evil spirits."

You're an evil spirit, I wanted desperately to say. But at least I had some good news for a change.

I glanced back at the jar of saffron. Hopefully, the magic of this place would transform the plastic bear into something more suitable for the king.

"You will also bring me a goat."

My head snapped back around.

"I'm sorry. What?"

I don't know whether King Tut repeated himself or not. It honestly, didn't matter. I heard him loud and clear that first time.

He wanted a goat.

A frickin' goat.

Saffron threads fit in an envelope and beneath the pedestal that held King Tut's urn with ease. I couldn't fit a goat under the museum display. But my thoughts were already too far ahead.

Where would I get a goat? And how would I convince my parents to bring it to the museum in the first place?

My stomach rumbled, but with anxiety instead of farts. This was an impossible task.

"I can bring you three jars of honey, but I can't bring you a goat."

King Tut's eyes narrowed, and my face burned red.

"Three *sacred* jars of honey."

There was another rumble, this one from the palace itself. My knees buckled as the earth quaked.

The cold stone floor rushed up to meet me.

Flames flickered as they choked on the dust falling from the ceiling.

Except I'd never seen dust fall that quickly.

I glanced up as a grain of sand bounced off my cheek.

Then the flood gates opened.

Sand rained down like an angry hourglass. A layer built up on the stone around me in a matter of heartbeats.

Grains filled my sneakers and buried my hands.

I scrambled to my feet and pressed my hand to my forehead, desperate to keep sand out of my eyes.

"I'm sorry! I'll get your goat!"

No response.

"I'll get you two goats!"

Sand clumped on the floor. I marched in place, trying to keep my legs free. It was no use.

Wind whipped up and sand fell faster. It made quick work of my ankles and raced toward my knees.

"Five goats!"

I lost sight of the Pharaoh in the sandstorm. Then, a brief gap appeared, and I located the throne.

The empty throne.

The pyramid shook with another a low rumble. Sand piled higher. Every struggled movement pulled me down faster as the sand covered my shoulders.

My cheek stung under the weight of something too meaty for sand.

"Aunt Lucil—"

Sand filled my mouth, cutting off my call for help.

I tried to spit but only swallowed the contents of the Sahara Desert.

My muscles ached as the weight of the sand pushed against my eyelids.

I stopped struggling. This was it. How I met my end.

Until something struck my opposite cheek.

The sand fell away as if the hourglass had been a giant toilet someone had finally courtesy flushed.

I gasped for air as the sensation of falling replaced that of suffocating.

"Get out of my nephew, you son of a..."

My eyes flicked open.

Aunt Lucille crouched over me, her hand inches away from slapping me again.

"I'm back." I threw my hands up to protect my sore face and got the most awkward high-five ever.

"Thank the gods." My aunt scooped me off the floor and cradled me in her arms. "I was so worried."

"Can't... breathe..."

Grains of sand gritted between my teeth with each word.

I spat onto the carpet and ran my tongue around my mouth. Clean.

Had I imagined it?

"Eww," she said, finally letting go. "What happened?"

I checked the corners of the room and took a deep breath. It smelled like Toot was long gone.

"Did you see him?" I asked, turning my attention back to my aunt.

"Your ghost?" She shook her head. "But I felt a dark presence. You said you'd be alright."

"Everything was fine until..."

"Until what?"

"I told Tut I couldn't bring him a goat. That made him angry. Like, topple his entire palace angry. He didn't even stop after I promised to bring him one."

Aunt Lucille stared.

"Or maybe five," I said with a frown.

CHAPTER 5
EXERCISING YOUR FARTS

"You what?" Aunt Lucille's eyes bulged out to the point where she looked like another cruel hallucination.

"You never make deals with otherworldly entities. That's spirit one-oh-one."

My normally easy-going aunt's nostrils flared, and I feared for a second that she might slap me again (Though she would never. Unless it was the only way to get me out of ancient Egypt, of course).

"I had to. He was going to bury me alive."

"It was just a threat. He wants something from you and wouldn't have let you die." She sank to the floor and shook her head. "No. No, no, no."

"I don't see why it's a big deal. I'm already cursed."

"This is bad. This is seriously bad." She shook her head for the umpteenth time.

But I still didn't get it. I guess I didn't know anything about spirits.

"You don't know anything about spirits, John."

See?

"Curses can be broken."

I nodded, following her so far.

"But something promised can't be unpromised. You entered into a contract with a malevolent force that's thousands of years old." → hateful

I blinked. "But I'm eleven. I can't drive or vote, how can I make a contract?"

Aunt Lucille stared into my eyes. "Do you think The Devil cares about what's legal?"

My heart quickened. Tut wasn't The Devil, but her concern finally made sense.

"No. I guess not."

"John..." She rose up on her knees and grabbed my shoulders. "Tell me *exactly* what you promised him. Word for word."

"Five goats and a jar of honey."

Aunt Lucille blinked.

"That's all?"

"Well... Maybe it was three jars of honey."

"You're sure?"

I nodded.

She dropped to her bottom again and muttered to herself.

"I can get you three jars of quality honey. But goats... Goats will be tricky."

My aunt leaned her head to one side and said nothing for a while. I presumed she's where I got it from—getting carried away with my own thoughts instead of paying attention to anything around me.

Eventually, she snapped back to reality, and I saw the focus return to her eyes.

"Okay. We're breaking into a petting zoo."

As I started imagining how exactly we'd do that, she licked her lips.

"Hang on," she said. "Did he specify *live* goats?"

Before I could protest the notion of sacrificing said goats, I saw the light bulb go on above her head.

"Wait. Did you negotiate a timeline? Sundown or something?"

I shook my head.

A sly smile broke out on her face. That was the aunt I remembered. "Good. Here's what we're going to do. You may have promised goats and honey but never agreed upon a delivery date. Provided you intend to do so at some point in the future, you're in the clear. For now, our priority remains breaking the curse."

"How do we do that?"

"Let me worry about that." Aunt Lucille grabbed my shoulders. "Just promise you won't make any more deals with ghosts."

The sensation of sand in my throat returned and kept me from responding.

"John?"

I nodded, hoping I'd be strong enough next time. Agreeing while in the comfort of my room was one thing. While sand filled every orifice, on the other hand...

"Good," she said, clapping her hands together. "Let me teach you a grounding ritual. Follow my lead."

The bracelets around Aunt Lucille's wrists tinkled together as she raised her hands above her head.

"Imagine your breath carries weight. That it squeezes any negativity inside your body downward as you exhale. Feel it condense it into a solid mass around your feet."

I followed my aunt's lead, lowering my arms while blowing out an imaginary birthday cake.

"Good. Again. Slower."

She took a deep breath before shutting her eyes, raising her arms, and repeating the movements.

I watched closely and followed along, taking about fifteen seconds to complete the movements.

"Focus on your breath," she said. "Slower still."

I closed my eyes and lost count of the amount of breaths I'd taken. My aunt said nothing, lost in the pitch-black behind our respective eyelids.

My breaths became less forced and the movement of my hands more fluid. Then I noticed something.

My pulse slowed.

My shoulders relaxed.

Maybe Aunt Lucille was on to something.

"Now," she continued. "We request that Mother Earth carry our burdens away."

She whispered something.

I strained my ears but couldn't make out anything she said. My breathing grew more hurried, and the calm slipped from my grasp.

"Done?" she asked.

My eyes popped open.

Wait. She hadn't asked for both of us? What was I even supposed to say?

Hey, Mother Earth, I know we don't talk much... or ever. Could you do me a favor and take these fart ghosts from me? Please?

"Great," continued Aunt Lucille. "Imagine opening a drain in your right leg and let all that negativity empty into the earth."

Aunt Lucille bounced in place, had her left leg flailing about like she was trying to shake a turd from her pant leg. Out from her skirt, whatever.

Try as I might, I couldn't contain my giggles. At least not until—

"AAAAAAH!"

My heart skipped a beat as she screamed at the top of her lungs.

"Go ahead. Let it all out," my aunt insisted.

A smirk formed at the corner of her lips.

She screamed again, not a bit quieter.

I clamped my eyes shut again and gave it my all.

"AAH!" I bucked my leg, giving that imaginary log in my pajama pants the ride of a lifetime.

It worked. A feeling of calm descended upon me once more.

Until the floor outside my room creaked. I expected Dad, ready with some kind of comment about Mom's sister being a crazy old bird.

Instead, there was a snicker.

I opened my eyes to find Leyla standing in the doorway, a kitten cradled in one arm and her cell phone in the other. "You guys are freaking weird."

My cheeks flushed red, and I planted both feet firmly on the ground.

"You better not be record—"

But my aunt had it covered.

"This is important, Leyla. I'll thank you not to interfere."

Aunt Lucille hooked her free leg around the door, swinging it closed. All without losing her balance.

"We're going to repeat this twice more. There's power in the number three."

But something burbled in my stomach. All the bouncing was as effective as those yoga "bowel" moves.

If I kept this up, I'd be the one going number three.

I practically snorted at my own joke and teetered to the side, nearly falling over.

"Umm, Aunt Lucille…"

"Yes?"

"Is it dangerous to pause the ritual once it's started?"

"Dangerous?" she asked, eyeing me. "Why?"

"Because I have to go to the bathroom."

My stomach rumbled. Loud enough for my aunt's ears, judging by how she retreated a step. "Go. We'll pick up where we left off."

I waddled to the bathroom praying I'd outpace the ancient Egyptian god of dookie.

And I'm proud to say I did. Or at least, I got the door shut before my backside mimicked a jet engine.

The bathroom mirror rattled. But on the bright side, nothing ran down my leg. Yet…

I hopped onto the toilet, but it was too soon for celebrations.

A complex scent of microwaved fish, rotting wood, and burnt toast snaked its way to my nose.

My face blushed. Aunt Lucille had probably heard all of that. Heck, she probably *smelled* it, too.

I stretched, reaching for the fan switch. Nope. My arm was about three feet short.

I lifted one cheek off the toilet, inching closer to the wall. Bad idea.

Another gust of wind bellowed from my bottom. It was every bit as powerful with one difference: the toilet bowl acted like a fart-megaphone.

The entire house shook.

The shower curtain billowed like a ship caught in a hurricane.

Car alarms went off all over the street.

I gagged as somehow the smell worsened. Mother Nature hadn't heard my prayer. Toot and company would show their transparent faces any second now.

A faint green haze seeped up from the gaps in the toilet. With my stomach mostly settled, I pulled up my pants, backed away and hit the fan switch.

The stink cloud swirled, undaunted. That fan wasn't rated for ghost dispersal.

Should I call my aunt? Could she banish the specter before it formed?

"Aun—"

I stopped, recalling my near-death experience. What would Toot do to her if he knew what I had planned?

Only one other logical solution.

I flushed.

The toilet gurgled, but I couldn't tell whether it pulled the funk down slightly, or if it was my imagination.

I pushed the lever again.

The toilet didn't react.

My thumb hammered on that silver knob like a pinball master struggling to save his last ball. The rubber flapper thudded within the empty tank, applauding my efforts.

I slammed the seat shut.

Stink seeped upward, unfazed.

Fingers crossed, I tried the lever one last time.

BAWOOSH!

But it was too little, too late.

The cloud lifted upward, growing and darkening by the second.

I threw open the sink cabinet, knocked over shampoo bottles looking for the air freshener. Nothing.

The cloud drifted past me and blocked the door. It became more defined, hazy edges hardening into distinct lines.

An unmistakable hat reflected in the mirror.

Curls.

And the face of an angry ghost that I had slammed a door on last night.

Perfect.

CHAPTER 6
FIGHTING FARTS WITH FARTS

Larry gave me an all-too toothy smile, his ghostly curls bouncing up and down as he floated in place.

Before he rushed in and wiped me from existence, I tried something drastic: the magic word.

"Please!" I said, holding my hands up. "Don't hurt me. It's not my fault you're here."

The edges of his face softened, and he kept his distance. "Where is here?"

"My home in Illinois. Now can you please leave me alone?"

"Illinois?" he murmured, looking around the bathroom.

He looked back at me again. The ridges on his brow wrinkled, and I felt compelled to elaborate.

"Well, you're in the bathroom of my house. Which is in Illinois."

"I don't understand."

Larry hovered closer to the mirror, half his body sticking through the cabinets.

This was my chance.

I kept an eye on him with my back against the wall, sliding closer to the door.

Larry didn't attempt to stop me, even when my fingers reached the doorknob. Before I turned it, I noticed something all too familiar in his eyes besides confusion.

Fear.

I sighed and let go. Larry was a victim of the curse, just like me.

"That's a mirror," I said. "That's your reflection."

"I know what a mirror is," said Larry, still inspecting himself in the pane of glass. "We had them in my time too. Do you know how closely guarded the secrets of mirror making was in the fifteen-hundreds?"

What?

I shook my head after a second, trying not to be rude.

"Incredibly. Craftsman risked assassination if suspected of sharing the knowledge with others."

I scratched my head. "Umm... Okay." That was the kind of weird fact Dad usually dished out.

"What I don't understand is how I got here." He looked down, as if just realizing his lower half was somewhere in our plumbing. "Am I dead?"

"Uhh..."

He floated my way again and I pressed even closer to the wall. I kicked myself for not running back to my aunt a minute earlier.

Larry paused and then floated back a "step."

"You're afraid of me," he said. His shoulders drooped. "It's because I'm dead."

"Well, not exactly."

The ghost crossed his arms over his chest, reminding me of Tut. But his gesture didn't have the same regal-feel.

"What do you mean?" He floated upward. "I couldn't fly when I was alive."

"You weren't ever alive. You're the mascot of a breakfast cereal company."

"Nonsense," he said. "I remember everything I knew in life. Like the fact that the Romans used urine imported from Portugal as mouthwash."

"Eww... What?"

(By the way, that's true. I looked it up later.)

"Or that ketchup was originally sold as a cure for diarrhea."

(Oddly, also true.)

"Hang on," I said. "These just sound like random weird facts off the internet."

Larry shook his head. "Nuh uh."

"Then tell me something personal. Or how you know what the internet is."

He stopped bobbing up and down and froze in place. As unnerving as it is seeing a ghost floating in front of you, it's even worse having one completely motionless.

I tried a different tactic.

"What was your favorite color? Or your favorite food?"

"Orange," the ghost said matter-of-factly.

"You're just saying that because it's both a fruit and a color."

"Nuh uh."

"Fine. Tell me the name of your best friend."

"Uhh..." Larry hung his head. "Orange?"

His form became more translucent.

I stared at the door again and sighed. "I'm sorry, Larry, but you're only here because I'm cursed."

The Quaker ghost removed his hat and held it over his heart. Color drained from his form (well, as much color as a black and white ghost had anyway) until I could barely distinguish him from the bathroom wall.

It wasn't my quirky aunt's 'magic' killing him, or air freshener, but the harsh reality of life (or lack thereof).

"What if we helped each other?" I blurted out as I noticed the tears running down his translucent cheeks.

His form solidified slightly, just as my aunt's warning about making deals with otherworldly entities played back in my head.

This was a unique opportunity I couldn't pass up. Larry was more than a victim. He was born of the curse itself and might have some insight.

"If you helped me break the curse, you'll gain your freedom."

The air shimmered for a second. Larry grew opaquer.

"Of course I'll help you, lad."

I did a double take. "Really?"

"Children are the greatest and most pure of God's gifts."

Oh, right... The Quakers were super religious.

"Umm... Exactly."

I took a deep breath. This was just a wild stab in the dark. First, I'd have to tell him the full story so he understood.

"I accidentally ate a wheel of cheese belonging to King Toot and he's holding me against my will."

"King who?"

I blinked. *He knew about ketchup and mirrors and Spanish pee, but not King Tut?*

"King Tutankhamun. The other ghost you saw last night. Before I... slammed the door on you. Sorry about that," I said with a shrug, but he ignored my apology.

"Ah. The fellow with the fancy headdress." He clicked his tongue. "The British sure adopted some weird cultures since I was... not alive."

I remembered that bit from the museum tour. Howard Carter didn't discover King Tut's until the early nineteen twenties—more than a hundred years after the oatmeal marketing team did their thing. Maybe he only knew stuff from before then.

"He's not that kind of king." I shook my head. "Well, he *is* that kind of king, just not British. Anyway, he won't remove his curse until I steal a bunch of things for him. I thought you could do something, since you're both ghosts? Can you remove the curse?"

His shoulders hunched and he floated closer.

"My religious beliefs prevent me from engaging in the proliferation of witchcraft." *spreading*

"I don't care *how* you stop him."

Larry scratched his head and replaced his hat. He didn't look too sure about things.

I put on a cheesy smile. "Kids are the future, right?"

He sighed and straightened his vest. "We have a deal. I'll see what I can do, my boy."

"Thank you!" I reached out, then remembered a hug held the potential to unmake me.

Larry's head jerked toward the hallway. His ghostly nostrils flared.

"What the dickens is that?"

His head and torso disappeared through the bathroom door.

I leaned toward the door and strained my ears, but it was the red streak in the mirror that drew my attention.

Strands of fire ran through Larry's form like burning steel wool (If you've never seen that, Google it).

Flames waged a silent war on my fart ghost.

Around the door.

The very *wooden* door.

I jumped to the faucet and flung handfuls of water around the room. The H-two-O splashed against the door.

The fire raged on, twisting and burning until my ghost was no longer transparent.

"Uhh... Larry?"

All at once, the inferno stopped.

Specks of ash floated in midair for a moment before winking out of existence.

Then I noticed what must have drawn Larry's attention in the first place.

An odd smell hung in the air. It hadn't come out of me. This one was something burning. Something earthy.

Smoke seeped into the bathroom from beneath the door.

"Toot?" I whispered.

Tears welled in my eyes. The smoke had a mind of its own. It snaked around and under the door, straight into my lungs.

My mind raced as I coughed.

Was this another aspect of the curse?

An additional ghost that slipped out with Larry? Someone who met their terrible demise in a fire?

We lived near Chicago, after all. Part of Mom and Dad's "moving transition plan" included watching a documentary on the city. It taught us about the Chicago Fire (The tragedy from the eighteen seventies, not the soccer team. And who names a sport's team after a tragedy that killed hundreds of people and destroyed several square miles of property, anyway?).

A fire started by a stupid cow knocking over a lantern.

I waved my hands, clearing the odd-smelling smoke from my face.

"John..." a ghostly voice echoed from the hallway.

Wait, ghost cows couldn't talk. Or could they?

A knock came on the door.

Ghost cows definitely didn't have knuckles.

I tapped the doorknob with the back of my hand. Cool to the touch. At least the house wasn't on fire. I gave it a twist and pulled the door open.

No cows.

Just Aunt Lucille.

She stood in the hallway, her hair tucked beneath a bandana to keep it safe from a burning bundle of herbs in her hand. In the other hand, she held the blue salt canister I'd seen her take out of her bag.

A thick layer of salt lined the bathroom threshold.

I coughed again and waved the smoke out of my face.

"You've been in there for a while, so I started smudging," she said.

"Smudging?" I asked, forgetting about Larry for a moment.

"Sage," she said, raising the smoking bundle of herbs.

I blinked. Well, that cleared up exactly nothing.

Noticing the confusion on my face, she gave me another lesson.

"Burning sage banishes negative spirits while inviting positivity into a space." She wrinkled her nose and backed up a step. "Even in the bathroom."

That sounded exactly like what I needed. Even if it stank.

"Okay. Well, I'm done in there."

Aunt Lucille kept her distance, waving smoke into the bathroom before following me into my room.

She lingered in each of the corners, lifting the smudge "stick" while muttering some kind of... prayer? Spell?

Crap.

My mind caught up with what had just happened.

She'd succeeded in killed Larry. Roasted him "alive" with her spirit-banishing smoke. And my best chance of breaking free from King Tut's curse burned up along with him.

Unless the smoke would work on him too? It seemed unlikely, but I recalled sage being in our spice rack.

I shuffled closer to Aunt Lucille in case those magic words were important.

She mumbled again after moving to the far corner.

"Ancestors, please protect John and his family." She stiffened and her voice grew more demanding. "I command the forces troubling him to leave this place. You are no longer welcome."

As she lifted the smoking herbs to the ceiling, something magical happened. A terrible screeching sound filled the room as her magic destroyed the bonds of my curse once and for all.

Or... you know, set off the smoke detector outside my room.

CHAPTER 7
BROKEN BONES AND PHARE-WOES

"Fire! Everybody up!" Dad yelled. (Still not sure how the smoke alarm woke him but me and my aunt's yelling earlier hadn't.)

A blur of hairy chest and boxers with little hearts flew past my door. He came back a second later with the fire extinguisher from the linen closet.

As soon as he saw his sister-in-law, he took a deep breath and bit his lip.

Aunt Lucille froze. Unfortunately, Dad's vision wasn't movement-based like the T-Rex.

That's when Mom showed up (wearing more clothes than Dad, thankfully).

"Never mind," Dad yelled, looking back at Mom. "It's just your sister smoking in the house."

Leyla showed up at the tail end of Dad's tirade, carrying a sleeping bundle of fur in her arms. "Eww, put on some clothes," she said before slamming her bedroom door.

Dad reached up on his tiptoes and pressed a button on the smoke detector. The loud screeching ceased, but so did his grip on the extinguisher.

The heavy metal container plummeted to the floor.

While Dad wasn't cursed, we shared a similar trend of luck. The extinguisher landed square on his toe before spurting white powder all over the wall.

Dad spewed a string of colorful obscenities and hopped around on his other foot.

"Are you okay?"

Aunt Lucille rushed forward and reached for his foot, unfortunately, forgetting about the burning bundle of herbs in her hand. 

Dad screamed again as hot embers singed the hair on his ankle.

"I'm fine!" he said, shifting weight to his other foot. "Just get away from me."

"I'm sorry," my aunt said. "It looks broken."

"Yeah. You think?"

A knife twisted in my gut.

I had my own problems. Stomach cramps sucked the wind from my lungs, doubling me over. This wasn't any ordinary pain.

More farts? Now?

"John, are *you* okay?" Dad asked, wincing as he hobbled toward me.

"Yeah." I forced myself upright and clenched my cheeks.

News flash. It didn't work.

I didn't make a jet engine noise this time. Instead, it went for a more cartoony slide whistle effect. The fart started low and rose in pitch right up until the end.

Everyone stared.

I took a risky sniff. Odorless.

Dad blinked. "Excuse me."

"Uh... Excuse me," I said.

My stomach still ached. The curse demanded maximum embarrassment. Because we all know what the word embarrass ends with...

"I'll drive you to the hospital," Aunt Lucille blurted out, taking the attention away from me.

"Thank you." He hopped away from her, using the railing for support. "I'll just drive myself."

Mom swooped in and took his arm. "I'll take you. Watch the kids, Luce?"

"Of course," Aunt Lucille said with a nod. "I'm sorry, Johnathan," she called out as my parents headed down the stairs.

Dad grumbled something, but all I made out was Mom's assurance that, "We'll all laugh about this one day."

My aunt and I stood in the hallway in awkward silence, the curse wreaking havoc in my belly.

"I'm going back to bed. I'm not feeling too—"

Thrrrrrrrrp.

Aunt Lucille jumped back just in time as the smell spread. This one was ripe. Like an overcrowded elephant enclosure on the hottest day in July.

"Oh my." She gagged and slipped the bandana from her hair over her nose.

My poor aunt. I'd been through this enough to know a thin piece of fabric wouldn't help.

I held my breath and tugged on my bedroom window. It screeched to a stop a mere two inches later.

Stupid child safety lock.

I fiddled with the little plastic stopper with one hand and feebly waved the gathering sink cloud outside.

Meanwhile, my aunt had turned a shade of green never seen on a person. She clamped her nose shut and fumbled with the various trinkets around her neck.

Sorry, Aunt Lucille, prayer won't help any more than that bandana.

But she finally found what she wanted: a tiny vial affixed to a twine cord. She uncorked it and flicked her wrist.

I prepared for the burning as holy water splattered my face. It never came, though, because I'm not a vampire.

Sniff, sniff...

And it was some kind of essential oil.

All it did was make the room smell like fresh-baked peppermint turd brownies. Granted, it was a slight improvement.

I cupped my hands and waved the stench out the tiny window slit.

As I did, the air solidified like it had in the bathroom. Greenish stick lines swirled before my eyes.

Too late.

An elaborate, gleaming headdress appeared in the middle of the room. A well-tanned, translucent face followed. King Toot floated upward. His arms crossed over his chest, one hand holding an ankh.

I couldn't do a thing other than marvel at how majestic the ghost of ancient Egypt's youngest ruler looked.

Toot wrinkled his nose. "It smells worse than a camel's bottom in here."

I cracked a smile and failed to hold back a chuckle. I didn't recall him having a sense of humor.

My laughter was short lived. Something about this made no sense. His royal heinie-ness was no stranger to my brand of tear gas.

Unless... It was the sage smoke hanging in the air, not the peppermint or the rancid fart.

My aunt and I stared at one another through Toot's translucent torso. In turn, my fart ghost watched us.

Any remnants of hope left the building.

My aunt knew her stuff. She'd bested Larry. However, ancient Egypt's most famous ruler was out of her league. Keeping her here only endangered her life.

Toot floated around my aunt, sizing her up.

He wasn't stupid. He had to understand her intentions. How long before he punished her too?

So, I did what I did best when it came to the curse. I lied.

"Did you see that?" I blurted out.

"See what?"

"The ghost... He just burned up in front of my eyes. The sage worked."

Technically I wasn't lying because I didn't specify *which* ghost.

I wrapped my arms around her.

Toot floated back, watching us intently.

"I'll get you your goats and honey," I whispered.

"You'd better," the ghost said as he descended through the floor.

My aunt pulled back and narrowed her eyes. "The spirits still have a plan for you, John. Of that, I'm sure."

"Well, that's why you gave me the cat, right?"

"Hmm... I suppose so."

I smiled. "You're only a call away if the ghost returns, right?"

Aunt Lucille nodded, still looking skeptical. She knew I wasn't being truthful. Adults always seem to know.

I had to get her out of my room.

"I feel better already." Before I could add, "I promise," my tummy rumbled, startling both of us.

"And that?" she said.

I looked down. "My belly demanding breakfast."

She laughed. "I can whip up some pancakes for you guys."

"That sounds delicious."

While my aunt went downstairs, I took the opportunity to complete my morning routine (getting dressed, teeth brushed, and so on). Then I grabbed my school laptop. I wasn't sure my friends could help, but they always had bright ideas, and it was nice not feeling alone.

The machine rang once... twice...

Park and Akira never answered. Following the third ring, Other John's face appeared on the screen.

If you need a refresher, John was the first friend I made after starting school. He, Akira, and Park all helped me pick up my belongings after I knocked over King Tut's vase.

Unfortunately, they were also the ones who slipped the cursed cheese in my lunch bag.

Becoming "Other John" was his idea for avoiding confusion. He wants to go back to just "John," but everyone thinks it's funnier this way.

His eyes were halfway open, and his hello was garbled by a drawn-out yawn.

"I need help," I said.

"Yeah. Professional."

"This is serious. I'm farting other ghosts now."

His eyes immediately gained focus, and he leaned closer to the camera. "Really? Who?"

"Just a stupid cereal mascot. The important part is that Larry agreed to help me get rid of Toot."

Other John shook his head. "Wait, who's Larry?"

"The *other* fart ghost. Keep up."

"You didn't say that." He yawned again. "I just woke up, man. If you found a helpful fart ghost, why do you need me?"

"That ghost is gone. My aunt got rid of it." I sighed. "It's a long story."

"Shorten it."

I scratched my head. "The food I eat determines who I fart out. So I need ideas."

"Psssh. Easy. Who would know all about curses?"

"Other than my aunt? I don't know. That's why I'm looking for ideas."

"Come on," Other John said. "It should be obvious."

It really wasn't. I sat there staring until he finally answered his own question.

"Witches."

"A witch? I don't know..." I said with a shake of my head. "Knowing my luck, I'll get one from a horror story. One that eats children."

He rolled his eyes. "Well, obviously you're not going to summon a fart witch that eats children. *You'd* have to eat a child to do that."

Ugh. I hated the fact that he was right.

"So, what do witches that *don't* eat children eat?"

"No idea," he said. "Live frogs?"

"I'm not eating a live frog."

"Hang on. I've got to take a whizz. Be right back." Other John disappeared, but I heard him off screen. "You shouldn't rule out eating a frog."

"I'M NOT GONNA EAT A FROG!"

"Okay…" came my aunt's voice from the doorway. "Can I come in?"

I sat up and nodded.

She stood at the edge of my bed.

"I came up to give you something, but now I'm concerned whether a dark entity is pressuring you to eat frogs."

I pointed at my laptop. "I'm on the phone with a friend."

"Ah…" Aunt Lucille said. I wasn't sure she believed me given the blank screen. She held out her hand, revealing a pointy rock.

"Crystal quartz. Another layer of protection."

Rainbows danced inside the crystal as I held it up to the light. If the sage didn't help, neither would a pretty rock. A rock indistinguishable from the others she'd given me over the years. I'd probably lost or thrown away at least a dozen.

"Thanks," I said, and stuffed the stone into my pocket just as she wrapped her arms around me.

"It came to me while peeing!" Other John announced. "Harry Houdini, the greatest magician."

My aunt pulled away. "He didn't eat frogs to my knowledge."

"This is my friend Other John," I said, and gestured to my aunt. "Other John, this is my aunt Lucille. We were arguing over the world's most famous magician."

"Living *or* dead," Other John clarified.

Smart. See why I kept him around?

"That depends." Aunt Lucille shifted her weight and stared off into the distance for a moment.

"There are so many different types of magicians. You've got your comedic acts, like Penn and Teller or The Amazing Jonathan. And then you have stage magic like David Copperfield or Kriss Angel. Then you have your historical figures, like Faust, Crowley, and Rasputin."

Okay. Historical is good.

"But those individuals dabbled in something darker."

Nope. Not so good.

"So not Houdini?" Other John asked.

"Well, Harry Houdini wasn't really known for his magic. He gained recognition as an escape artist."

I perked up.

An escape artist was exactly what I needed.

My aunt shared her knowledge about magicians, which we quickly ignored. Other John's face disappeared. Replaced by a questionable picture.

Before I could ask him why he'd shared a picture of a plate of poop, I noticed the caption:

Hungarian chicken paprikash with spaetzle.

And the search bar:

Harry Houdini's favorite food.

This was my chance.

"I think you're right, Aunt Lucille. It's Houdini."

Before she could argue, I angled the laptop in her direction.

"I've been thinking about this morning and how we can make things up to Dad. Cooking his favorite meal might get you back on his good side."

Don't judge me. Yes, it was terrible after all my aunt had done for me and I still feel bad. But I didn't know what else to do at that point. And Hungarian Chicken sounded like something Dad would have liked.

Even if it looked like it had already been chewed and pooped out.

CHAPTER 8
FARTSTORMING

Instead of boring you with the rest of the weekend, I'll give you the highlights.

Mom and Dad spent five hours in the ER. Dad had two broken toes but luckily didn't need surgery. He did, however, get some decent painkillers. Painkillers that let him gloss over the fact that his favorite meal was "Chicken Paprikash" and not "tacos or anything taco adjacent."

He forgave Aunt Lucille, she headed home, and we wound up keeping the cat.

The most important takeaway was that our plan failed. Saturday night and Sunday passed without farting out any famous escape artists. Even after eating leftovers (which looked even *more* like dookie).

Our story picks back up at school on Monday morning.

Something sharp stabbed me in the thigh as I plopped down at my desk.

"Oww…"

I dug the quartz point out of my pocket, set it on my desk, and rubbed my leg.

Other John slid into the seat to my left.

"What's that?" he asked.

"Quartz. For protection."

A girl with long, straight black hair took a seat on the other side of me. Akira—one half of the twins.

"That won't help," she said.

"What?"

Akira sighed. "You're the one with the curse. How have you not done any research on King Tut?"

"I've done a little."

She stared.

I bit my lip. "I've been busy, okay."

Her twin brother Park took a seat behind her. He shared the same dark hair, though cut short to his scalp.

"I told you he wouldn't have," Park said.

"And I told you I wasn't taking that bet," Akira snapped back. She turned to me. "Do you even want to beat this curse?"

"Of course."

Akira leaned over and placed a circle of fabric on my desk. "Then start with this."

I picked up the patch embroidered with a golden bug.

"If you want to fight an ancient curse, you need to use ancient magic."

The patch didn't look any more impressive than my aunt's crystal. "How will a picture of a bug help?"

"It's not a bug," Park said.

"It's a scarab," Akira finished.

I blinked.

"You don't know what a scarab is?"

"Think giant beetle," piped in her brother.

Akira sighed. "They were a symbol of protection and safe passage in Egyptian culture. I thought putting it on your backpack would help."

"Thanks. I wish I knew how to sew."

"I can take care of that!" Other John snatched the patch out of my hand and reached into his fishing vest. From one of the dozens of vest pockets, he produced a mini stapler.

With two quick punches, my backpack had protection. At least, theoretically.

Other John twirled the stapler around his knuckles. And by twirled, I mean it made a half rotation before falling to the floor and launching a staple across the room.

I could see what he was going for, though, and it looked cool in my head.

"Thanks." I said, handing the tiny stapler back. "But I can't wear my backpack all the time."

"What if you got a scarab tattoo?" Park suggested.

"Mom won't even let me use colored hair spray."

"She doesn't have to know." Other John patted his chest. "Shoot. The tattoo ink is in my other vest."

I laughed.

"Tomorrow, then," he said with a smile.

My laugh tapered off. Was he serious? None of us knew what he kept in all those pockets.

Up until now, I wondered if it might have been magic, summoning whatever he required.

Sigh. If only it could whip up a goat.

I ran my finger over the fluffy patch and set my bag on the floor. "Thanks guys. I've been busy researching Quakers and magicians and making stupid deals to bring Tut honey..."

A girl in a flowery dress slid into the desk in front of me. I lowered my voice now that we had company.

Park and Akira met eyes, and I remembered that we hadn't conferenced them into our call.

"I ate a ton of granola bars and farted out the Quaker Oatmeal guy."

"What?" the twins said together.

"John's like a superhero. Nay... A pooperhero. He can fart anyone he puts his mind to," Other John said, throwing his hands in the air. "It's awesome."

Our classmates turned and stared.

"Shhh..." I said, covering my eyes.

It took a moment, but eventually everyone returned to their own business, and I continued. "Other John and I thought farting out Harry Houdini could help me break the curse."

"Okay," Akira said. "That's actually pretty smart."

"But he didn't show up after I ate his favorite meal."

"That's okay," Other John said. "I have backup plans."

He reached into his backpack and waved a piece of paper in the air. "I did my own research into which ghosts he should fart next."

He cleared his throat.

"First off, Archie Karas."

The name meant nothing to me. When I glanced at the twins, they shared my confusion.

Park beat me to it. "Never heard of him."

"He's one of the most famous gamblers in the world."

Akira blinked. "How is that going to help?"

"Uh... John could take a casino for all they're worth and buy back all of King Tut's artifacts. Plus, rich kids don't have to go to school."

"Half of Tut's artifacts are in museums and aren't for sale," said Akira. "And—"

Other John ignored her and continued down his list.

"Alexander Andreev. Russian Theoretical Physicist extraordinaire."

"Wha—"

"And inventor of the jetpack." He soared the paper through the air like an airplane. "Can you imagine flying with fart power?"

His excitement got the best of him and several classmates turned around. Only, they stared at me.

It's my second official day of fifth grade and I'm already the fart kid.

Other John didn't even notice.

"King Midas. Get some of that golden touch." He picked up a pencil and scratched the name out. "On second thought, golden dumps sound painful."

He let the pencil drop. "Why do they call it taking a dump, anyway? You're clearly leaving one."

Akira's eyes, well her whole face really, took on that "disappointed mother" look. "John, enough."

She reached over me and ripped the paper out of his hands. After glancing at it, she crumpled it up. "This is all garbage."

"Fine, but I'm John again!" Other John jumped up from his chair. "You guys heard her. No take backs."

He pointed at me. "Now he's Other John."

"Hmm..." Park looked at him and tilted his head. He gave it a shake. "Nope."

"Not happening," Akira said.

Mrs. Barwick stood from her desk and looked our way. Between that and the school bell, Other John composed himself and took his seat.

The bell went silent and the intercom next to the clock crackled.

"Today is Monday the nineteenth—" rattled off the assistant principal's voice.

I kept an eye on our teacher and whispered to the twins, filling them in more. "My aunt knows about magic and stuff. But she couldn't break the curse. I thought a magician could."

"Escape artist," Other John said. "Remember?"

"Is your aunt a witch?" Park whispered.

"Sort of," I said. "I guess."

"Did she tell you to stand in a salt circle when you fart?"

"No..."

"He can't carry salt with him everywhere," Akira snapped. "Sometimes I think you're as dense as Other John."

I sat up a little straighter upon remembering the line of salt in the carpet. Did that destroy Larry and not the sage?

"Hey!" Other John said loudly.

Mrs. Barwick stood up and gave him another angry glare. It was a shame that none of us had that power over him.

Someone on the other side of the room giggled, and our teacher shifted her attention.

Other John leaned closer and lowered his voice again. "There are no stupid ideas when you're brainstorming."

"True," said Park. "Fill your underwear with salt."

"Sounds... scratchy."

"Or light them on fire," Other John suggested.

"His underwear?" Park asked.

Other John turned and talked around me. "No. His farts. They're flammable. I'm suggesting he light the ghosts on fire before they form."

"That could work." Park nodded. "But I'd worry about singeing my—"

"Eww…" Akira clamped her eyes shut. "Stop talking."

Putting salt or fire near my butt sounded like a bad idea. I had to find a way to force Houdini to show up.

I slid my laptop from my bag and double-checked Other John's suggestion. Chicken Paprikash *was* Houdini's favorite dish.

My friends leaned in to see my screen.

"I thought that didn't work," Park said.

"It didn't," I said while typing out a search in another tab. "But maybe my aunt didn't cook the dish right."

I clicked on the first link.

"But Taste of Hungary looks authentic. The restaurant is only a thirty-minute drive. I just need someone who'll take us there."

Other John cleared his throat loudly.

But I was on a roll and mistook it for phlegm instead of the universal cue for "Someone's right behind you." Or in my case, right in front of me.

"Maybe if I ate dinner in a pair of handcuffs or a straitjacket—"

"Ahem," Mrs. Barwick said, tapping her heel on the floor.

It wasn't until then that I realized she'd been hovering over me this whole time.

"Mr. Pahrsink," she said.

"Uhh... Yeah?"

"Please stand."

I looked back at my friends and got to my feet.

"Would you recap this morning's announcements for your classmates that weren't paying attention."

A lump formed in my throat.

"Umm... it's Monday and it's going to be cloudy?"

It may sound like a stupid guess, but that was the gist of last Friday's announcements. That and an official welcome to all the new students.

Mrs. Barwick turned to address the rest of the room.

"Since your classmate is particularly interested in famous illusionists, he'll be doing magic for the school's talent show."

I blinked.

"What?"

As if public humiliation wasn't enough, my stomach decided it was time for backflips. I doubled over in pain.

The pain of you-know-what.

I clenched my cheeks, knowing full well it wouldn't hold back what was coming.

My friends shared a worried glance. Even they knew this wasn't a case of nerves.

I opened my mouth, but before I could say "bathroom" or even "nurse," pain drove me to my knees. I grabbed for my desk hoping to avoid landing on my face.

No such luck.

The abrupt meeting between my stomach and the floor forced the air from my lungs. The fart I'd been holding in escaped like a hot air balloon falling apart at the seams.

I shut my eyes and imagined my tombstone.

John Pahrsink.

Farted in class. Died of embarrassment.

But I didn't die.

And nobody vomited or screamed in horror.

Huh?

I knew I farted, but it came without thunderous applause.

Sniff. Sniff.

And by some miracle no smell?

I was in the clear. Still, the pain persisted. Pain that meant more gas to pass. I needed to get away from all these innocent bystanders.

Leaving my hand on my belly, I got back to my feet and looked up at my teacher.

"Bathroom..." is all I said.

Mrs. Barwick opened her mouth, and I feared she'd deny my request. But something in her eyes recognized the look of gastrointestinal distress.

"Make it quick," she said with a nod. "Before we begin today's lesson."

"Yes, Mrs. Barwick."

I broke into a sprint, dodging desks and backpacks alike.

As I passed Buttcrack Steve, the class bully, he grinned and stuck out his foot.

I'd been waiting for it, though and hurdled it with grace. With the teacher's back still turned, I couldn't help but stick out my tongue as I grabbed the door handle.

An ear-shattering rumble erupted from the back corner of the classroom.

Akira's hair—well, every kid in the class with long hair—blew sideways from the epicenter of the blast.

A heat wave roared over me. My ears rang and my vision went white. That fart wasn't silent after all...

CHAPTER 9
SMOKE AND MIRRORS

My vision slowly returned, revealing a thick cloud of smoke where my desk had been. It billowed outward, creeping toward my friends.

That was bad.

No. Not bad. Catastrophic.

I guess time was up. The Pharaoh wanted his offerings.

Neither Akira nor Park moved a muscle.

My eyes flicked to the floor. Just like the sand in Tut's palace, smoke consumed their feet. And then their legs.

Other John had crouched on his chair, safely out of reach of the paralytic fog. For now...

His hands searched through the endless array of vest pockets, probably looking for a perfume bottle. Would that even work against... whatever that was?

Meanwhile, the rest of the students giggled, oblivious to the danger.

I had to do something. Would a vacuum from the janitor's closet work against curse smoke?

I couldn't risk my friends' lives on a dusty old appliance. The only way out of this was to give Tut what he wanted.

That's when the light bulb went off.

My teachers in Ohio always drank tea. I'm sure it was no different here. Old people loved that stuff, especially with milk and honey. There had to be honey in the teacher's lounge.

I glanced back at my friends.

Other John had a tiny spray bottle in-hand ready to strike. He seemed to know more about this ghost fighting business than me. After all, it had been his idea to blast Toot with an air freshener.

I had to trust he'd keep the curse at bay until I got my hands on some bee vomit.

Before I could turn and leave, the smoke dropped like a ton of bricks and dissipated. In its place stood a dark-haired man dressed in a suit and bow tie. Well, not so much stood as floated.

The ghost whipped his hand out and a fancy black top hat materialized.

"Tada!"

Even from the door, his intense eyes matched those on my laptop screen.

I flung the door open. "Don't shoot, it's Houdini!"

Everyone turned and stared at me again.

Buttcrack Steve jumped up, and his chair clattered to the floor. He waved his hand in front of his nose. "More like Poodini."

"Sorry," I said, as Mrs. Barwick marched our way. "Bathroom."

Wait. What was I doing? I thought as the door clicked shut behind me.

The Chicken Paprikash summoned Houdini. That was what I wanted.

I peered through the glass strip of the door, hoping to motion for him to join me in the hall.

My friends had huddled together, no doubt discussing my latest ghost.

Mrs. Barwick paced back and forth, struggling to regain control of the class.

But where was my fartgician?

"Houdini?" I whispered, as I crept around the empty corridors of the school.

I stopped in the middle of the hallway.

Akira was right. I hadn't done enough research. Houdini wasn't the man's real name. But for the life of me, I couldn't remember what it was.

To spare you from homework, it was Erik Weisz. He chose the stage name "Houdini" after Jean-Eugene Robert-Houdin. He was another famous magician.

Because before video games came along, kids were stuck settling for having a favorite magician.

Dripping water echoed from the boy's bathroom as I continued my search.

The motion-activated lights were already on, but nobody stood before the urinals. And the mirror showed all the stall doors open.

"Tut?" I called out.

Nothing other than the sound of dripping water.

"Houdini?"

I followed the noise to the big, handicapped stall.

"Hou—"

I should have called for a plumber.

Water filled the bowl to the brim.

Blub.

I jumped as an air bubble broke on the surface. Water cascaded onto the floor as more and more bubbles floated up from the pipes.

The lights flickered and a dark cyclone swirled in the water.

My mind flashed back to the other day when Toot had turned Buttcrack Steve into a human puke fountain in this very bathroom. I didn't want to be here anymore.

Toilet water rained around me as a burlap sack wrapped in chains shot from the porcelain throne. It squirmed for a few seconds, like a butterfly shedding its cocoon.

Before I could throw my hands up to protect my face, the bindings splintered into a million pieces.

I shut my eyes and waited for the shrapnel to cut me to bits.

Drip.

Drip.

What followed was a severe lack of tiny bits of metal shredding my face. Don't get me wrong, I wasn't angry. Just confused.

I peeked through my fingers.

Airy Poodini floated before me, tuxedo perfectly dry and hair slicked back like he hadn't just risen from a middle school crapper.

My outfit, though? Plenty damp.

"Phew," I said. "I feared Other John got you with the perfume."

Poodini smoothed a non-existent wrinkle from his coat and looked down his nose at me. "The world's greatest escape artist? Never."

You want his help, dummy. Flatter the man.

"No," I said with a shake of my head. "Of course not."

He bobbed up and down without saying another word.

I looked down at my shoes and realized Akira had a point. Preparedness and I didn't go hand in hand.

"Mr. Houdini, you're the greatest mag... er... escape artist in the world."

Poodini's ghost rolled his eyes. "You say that like I'm unaware."

"That's why I called upon you for help."

"Yes... Yes... Obviously."

I scratched my head.

"I need your help, sir. With magic."

The magician's ghost snorted. "You don't have the gumption to be a great magician." He floated forward. I kept perfectly still as his wispy figure circled around me three times.

"I can't teach you to pull rabbits from hats or separate interlocking rings. You'll have to navigate your little talent show by yourself."

"I don't need your help for the talent show. Well, I probably do, but that's not why I called you."

I cleared my throat. "I need *real* magic."

He looked around the empty stall, then leaned closer. "I hate to break it to you kid, but magic isn't real."

"But..." I blinked. "You're a magician."

"No, I'm an escape artist." His chest puffed out and he stared straight through me. "Holding my breath impossibly long. Slipping straightjackets and cuffs. Defying death.

"I was never good at sleight of hand. Until now, I suppose." He pulled up his sleeves and waved a translucent hand in front of me. A fanned deck of cards appeared out of nowhere.

With a flick of his thumb, they whistled past my head one at a time.

Each sharpened card slammed against the metal door in rapid succession. I'd like to tell you that I didn't flinch or scream, but I did both those things (in addition to nearly falling over).

When I backed away from the door, a perfect outline of my body remained.

"See?" I said, trying to grab the four of hearts. The card slipped right through my fingers. "*That* was magic. You're a ghost. You can float through walls and change your appearance and break out of chains."

Poodini shrugged. "True. But that magic isn't available to *you*."

I took a deep breath. "I don't want you to teach me magic. I want you to use your magic to help me escape a curse."

Poodini flicked his wrist, and a wand appeared. With another flourish, sparks washed over me.

"Done," he said with an exaggerated wink.

"Really? Just like that?"

He sighed.

"Curses aren't real." Poodini gestured at himself. "I should know—I dedicated the last years of my life to disproving so-called psychic mediums and spiritualists."

"Would it matter if a person didn't curse me?"

Poodini raised an eyebrow.

"It was the ghost of King Tut."

He sucked in a sharp breath of air.

"*King Tutankhamun* cursed you?" Unlike Larry, his voice carried a hint of recognition. "What did you do, rob his tomb?"

"Ye—" I stammered. "Well, no. I mean... Not exactly."

"You're too young to have been there when Carter discovered King Tut's resting place." He eyed me. "It was all over the news a few years before I died, and that was a century ago. How did you run afoul of the Pharaoh's ghost?"

"I broke one of his vases and ate his cheese." I'd explained so many times that the words came without hesitation. "Now I fart ghosts."

Poodini's jaw dropped.

"You mean..." He looked down at his hands. "The world's greatest escape artist came out of your butt?"

"I'm afraid so. But not by choice."

He jabbed a ghostly finger dangerously close to my face. "You summoned me. I'd say that was by choice."

Darn. He had me there.

The illusionist's ghost hovered in place. "No matter. I will help you unravel this curse."

My eyes lit up. "Really?"

"But first, you'll give me something in exchange."

"Anything," I blurted out, forgetting Aunt Lucille's warning about making deals with spirits. Again.

"Your talent show act. Make it good enough to impress me."

And with that, his gaseous form dissipated like it came. In a cloud of smoke

CHAPTER 10
MAGIC FOR DUMMIES

Remember that stupid "I've got your nose" trick every parent plays on their child? That was the only trick I knew. That wouldn't impress anybody, let alone one of the greats.

But I had no choice.

Not only had I made *another* deal, but I'd done it without understanding the full terms. Poodini hadn't specified what would happen if I failed.

Tut made me his servant. Would Poodini do the same? An image of me in a red sequin dress being sawed in half popped into my head.

I shook the scene away. At least I'd have a partner of my own. After returning from the bathroom, Other John volunteered to be my assistant. Granted, he wasn't even familiar with the whole nose-stealing bit.

I was in for the longest week of my life...

"Hi, honey," Mom called from somewhere upstairs as I shut the front door. "How was your day?"

I grunted a response, slipped off my shoes, and ran to the bathroom. (Don't worry, it was only a number one). When I got out, the house was all mine.

Dad had another few hours of teaching at the university and Leyla got home from school fifteen minutes after me.

That meant the computer was free. Along with an entire internet's worth of magic tutorials.

I plopped down into the chair and pulled open the internet browser.

Easy magic tutorials.

The first video seemed most promising. "Level 1 to 100. Magic Tricks Anyone Can Do."

After a boring introduction, one of two guys flicked a lighter and transferred the flame to the fingertip of his opposite hand. He waved his burning finger in front of the camera before passing it back to the lighter and blowing it out.

That was awesome, I thought. *And it'd look amazing on a dark stage.*

The trick was simple. He had a second, slim lighter hidden behind his finger with a small rubber band.

Except I couldn't get away with bringing a lighter to school, much less two.

Bummer.

On cue, they transitioned to something else. A trick everyone my age already knew: "pulling" your thumb off your finger. Sure, the showmanship was better, but that one wouldn't impress anyone. It was no different than the dumb nose thing.

By the third trick, they'd already reached level thirty. Regardless of their poor counting ability, this one was cool. The man in the video made a playing card disappear and reappear out of thin air.

Even better, it didn't require any flammable materials. Instead, the card gets hidden on the back of your hand.

This went on for a while, so I won't waste your time narrating the entire video. Feel free to set the book down and watch it yourself if you're *that* interested. Just promise you'll come back.

The key take away is that it wasn't a hundred tricks, it was ten tricks, counting the levels by ten. False advertisement, for sure. But I did learn something.

The video left me with four tricks, probably not enough to fill out our allotted time. But if Other John prepared four tricks of his own, there was hope.

Time would tell whether ten minutes of amateur magic would impress Poodini.

"It better," I said aloud with a sigh.

By the time I got out of my own head, the next video had begun playing.

A man in a red shirt threw a shirt on a hanger into the air (that one was blue). He took a step forward, and somehow the blue shirt wound up on his body. He bent over, picked up the hanger, and hung it in the closet.

I rewatched the video several times. Even at half speed I couldn't figure out the trick. Worse yet, he provided no explanation. I scratched my head as the next clip rolled.

And then another.

Zach King was even better than Houdini. The only problem was that he didn't reveal the trick. Slowing down the videos was no help. After witnessing a puddle on the street swallow him whole, I realized something.

He was a human like me who possessed real magic.

The magic of video editing.

I sank back into the chair and sighed. Digital effects didn't work live on stage. But there was something Zach could teach me. His showmanship and smile were infectious.

"Do you have any homework?" Mom asked, stopping in front of the computer with a basket full of laundry in her hands.

"I'm doing it." I looked back at the screen and realized I wasn't. Zach now sat at a picnic table, dressed in winter gear. As he slammed his head into the table, he seamlessly turned into a pile of snow (wearing the same hat and coat, of course).

"Sort of," I said under my breath.

That's when I noticed the time. An hour had passed, and I hadn't so much as practiced a smile.

"Dinner will be ready in five," she said. "Please wash up and set the table."

With a sigh, I shut off the monitor and started toward the kitchen.

Yeah, I could have gotten another ten minutes or so before Mom got really angry, but I needed her on my side. Especially since I didn't know whether my teacher had sent home a note about my behavior.

Instead of boring you with the details of setting the table and putting out vitamins for everyone, I'll skip ahead to mealtime.

"How was school today?" Dad asked while covering his meatloaf in a thick layer of barbecue sauce.

I rolled peas around my plate while my brain did its little self-destructive dance.

What kind of ghost would peas summon?

How about Mom's famous breaded meatloaf?

The idea of some historical figure with ties to a brick of meat was crazy. But Larry wasn't real either. What if the curse did its thing regardless?

My imagination conjured a monstrosity of living meat leaving behind a grease trail as it lumbered toward me.

I dropped my fork and shoved the plate back a few inches.

No. That was ridiculous. I should have been worrying about more realistic things.

Like whether there was a limit on how many ghosts I could fart at a time.

Whether the next ghost in line would replace Houdini. And if it did, how would I get the escape artist back so he could help me?

My stomach grumbled and I couldn't ignore it any longer. Similar thoughts had kept me from eating lunch at school. Grilled cheese or pizza. Both reminded me of the Tut's wheel of cheese.

"That good, huh?" someone asked.

"What?" I looked up from my plate and glanced around the table, trying to figure out who'd spoken.

It was impossible since my whole family stared at me.

"Huh?"

"Leyla's trying out for the lead in the school play," Dad said. "I asked about your day."

"Dad, do you know anything about magic tricks?"

"Ah..." he said, lifting his chin. "It all makes sense now. You're distracted by a girl."

"What? No."

"Are you sure? Because magic is sure to impress the girls."

Leyla laughed.

"Stop," Mom said, shaking her head. "Girls do not like magic."

"I beg to differ. My buddy Pete taught himself magic in high school. Pulling coins out of thin air, card tricks, that kind of thing. He was good, and the girls loved it."

I shook my head. "Dad, this isn't about girls. I have to do a magic act for the school's talent show."

Dad raised an eyebrow. "But you don't know anything about magic."

"I know. That's why I asked. Did your friend show you the secret behind any of his tricks?"

"No. He didn't want any competition. Besides, it takes months, if not years of practice to get good at that stuff. Why don't you pick something you're already good at?"

"He's not good at *anything*," Leyla said.

Mom shot her the evil eye.

I ignored my sister. "It *has* to be magic."

Dad shrugged. "Then at least do a humorous magic performance. You'll only need half the number of tricks."

"Hmm..."

While my classmates would appreciate that, I doubted Mrs. Barwick had a sense of humor. And then there was Poodini. Would he feel cheated?

But with so little time it was my only shot.

"Maybe. Thanks, Dad."

He took a sip of his iced tea and set the glass down. "You know... Pete's coming into town and we're grabbing lunch on Thursday. I can ask him to bring some of his old props."

"The talent show is Thursday."

My stomach grumbled. Starving myself wouldn't lift the curse. And it certainly wouldn't help me focus on learning those tricks.

I picked up my fork and dug in.

The meatloaf.

The mashed potatoes.

The peas.

All of it. I finished dinner in record time without concern regarding their respective ghosts.

"Leyla, please clean up the table," Mom said.

My sister groaned. "That's John's job."

"He has magic to practice."

"Thanks, Mom," I said with a smile.

I placed my plate beside the sink, but Leyla still gave me the stink eye. I grabbed a deck of Marvel superhero playing cards from the game cabinet and ran up to my room.

Making a card appear from thin air looked easy. You tuck the corners between the fingers on the back of your hand. With a quick flip of your thumb and some flourish, you pass it to the front. Poof. Magic.

"Oh right... Jokes first." I watched myself shuffle the cards in my dresser mirror while trying to think.

Dad had a million horrible jokes. But did any of them fit the theme?

Ooh. Got one.

"How is a pack of cards like a pack of wolves? They both come in packs."

Half the cards slipped through my fingers and recarpeted my floor.

Ugh. Botched not once, but twice.

I stared at my reflection.

"How are wolves like playing cards? They both travel in packs."

That was it.

I shuffled the remaining cards and told the joke again, this time adding a goofy grin.

Getting better. It was almost funny. Now to focus on the trick itself.

I flipped over the top card and the remainder of them joined their family on the floor.

The Ace of Spades...

The death card (As pointed out by Aunt Lucille every time she played a card game).

Silly, right? It was just a piece of plastic-coated paper. But it *was* an omen.

After an hour of trying, I couldn't make the trick work. My hands were too small to reliably shuffle, much less hide a card behind.

Guess that was why there were no ten-year-old professional magicians. With a sigh, I crouched down for a trick I could do. Fifty-two-card pickup.

Turns out I had some magic in me after all. There was no stomach pain warning, just a rancid fart that sounded suspiciously like *ta-da*.

Great. Poodini was coming to laugh at me.

Time slowed as I turned my head and prepared an explanation for my failure.

"A debt must be paid," came a familiar ghostly voice.

Toot's telltale headdress zipped toward me, and my world went black.

CHAPTER 11
LOST IN TIME

Musty air tickled my nose, and I rose from the cold stone of King Tut's palace. The Pharaoh sat on his throne, gold glinting in the torchlight.

Something was different about him. Probably the enormous serpent-shaped staff with glowing emerald eyes that stared into my very soul.

Was he getting stronger?

"Ushabti..."

I gulped and brushed off my... dress? Well, it wasn't really a dress, but a Shendyt. Which is a length of cloth tied around the waist like a kilt.

King Tut's eyebrows had those sharp, dagger-like slants. I bowed, ignoring my newfound knowledge of ancient Egyptian fashion.

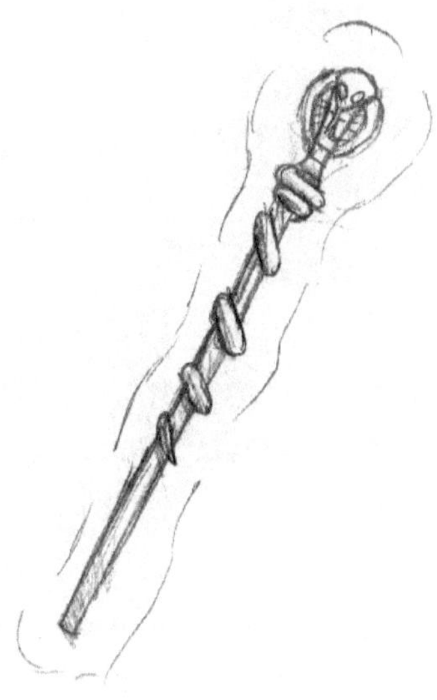

"I'm sorry I haven't delivered your honey yet," I said (in perfect Egyptian, I might add).

"Or my goats."

"Or your goats… But I'm working on it. I prom—"

A crack echoed as he rapped the staff against the floor.

"Eep."

"They can wait," he said, his features softening.

"They can?"

"Instruct your brother to serve as my vizier, and I will consider your entire debt clear."

I straightened up.

My entire debt?

"You'll remove the curse?" I stammered.

Tut nodded.

"Deal!" I shouted.

Whoops. There I go again…

"Wait. I don't have a brother."

"Erik."

Erik? I'd heard that name before.

Houdini! He meant my newest fart ghost.

I froze.

The way Tut's lips broadened told me he knew the internal struggle brewing in my mind. Poodini had agreed to help me, but my magic skills sucked with a capital 'S.' And what would he do after learning I planned on selling him out?

But what would Tut do if I refused?

"I'll do it."

"Good," Tut said. "He commands power I've not seen before. He will serve me well."

"You've... seen him?"

"He visited my palace, showed me wondrous things." King Tutankhamun's smile disappeared. "It displeased me when he declined my offer. But my Ushabti will change his mind."

Uh oh.

I paced in front of my lone contribution. A single golden jar full of spice. The table was big enough to hold dozens of jars. Plus dozens of whole cooked goats with room to spare. And that was just the table.

The palace itself had space galore. And Tut had untold amounts of goods stolen: gold, jewels, leather, furs.

What if he asked me for something that no longer existed?

Having the curse lifted was the only option. I had to convince Poodini to serve as Tutankhamun's new Ushabti.

Vizier, corrected an annoying voice in my head. But if Houdini had the guts to stand up to the King of Egypt, what chance did I have?

Then I'd have to find a way to trap him. Maybe fart him out into a bottle next time I got stomach cramps.

That was the moment the voice in my head reminded me that a simple glass bottle wouldn't hold a ghost.

A smarter move meant playing both sides. Go forward with the magic show and learn Poodini's escape plan before mentioning him serving Tut.

But I had to be careful. My butt was always within earshot. There was no telling what Poodini's ghost could hear.

The man seemed smart. Like *really* smart. After all, he'd found his way to whatever part of the ghostly world where Tut's palace resided.

Poodini was more than an illusionist. He had power. Even Tut confirmed that. Because more importantly than getting here, he'd found a way *out*.

I walked the perimeter of the room, running my fingers over sandstone blocks as large as Mom's SUV. I'd seen ghosts floating right through walls and doors but that didn't apply here. Heck, Tut had actual feet.

Fire roared in the golden braziers with their ever-burning firewood. The Pharaoh's butt didn't fall through the throne. When I'd first arrived, he hadn't bobbed up and down midair. He'd walked toward me in the sand like any other physical being.

King Tutankhamun ruled this place. He wanted Houdini as his advisor. He wouldn't have simply let him float through a wall and leave.

Poodini was the key.

First, I had to get home.

I turned and looked back at Tut. He watched from his towering throne.

Why was I still here?

Tut had made his demands, and I'd agreed to them. That should have been it.

I wandered back in front of the Pharaoh.

He didn't budge.

"So..." I tapped my hands against my side. "I'll bring you Poo—"

Tut raised the staff, and I swore the snake's eyes flashed red.

"My brother!" My eyes clamped shut. "And honey. And goats."

Stop talking, John.

The dull thud of staff on stone echoed throughout the pyramid.

That should have done it.

Except when I peeked out of my right eye, I was still inside the sandstone prison.

I closed my eyes so tightly they hurt.

My body, my *real* body, wasn't in Tut's palace. It lay on the floor of my bedroom on a carpet of playing cards.

I pictured the scene as hard as I could and opened my aching eyes.

Still in Egypt.

I wandered back to the spot in front of the throne in case I needed to be in the same spot as when I arrived.

Okay. When I farted, I was in this kind of pose.

I bent over, pretending to pick up imaginary cards. No matter how many times I blinked, my room didn't appear.

Tut wouldn't let me wish my way out of here.

"You can send me back anytime now..." I mumbled as I stood back up.

The Pharaoh smirked, suggesting he'd heard me. But that was all.

The monster had been keeping me there on purpose.

I couldn't figure out why. Trapping me here meant he didn't get what he wanted either.

Unless... Did he expect me to fart out Houdini then and there?

I took a deep breath and held it.

Okay. No big deal. You just have to fart on command. In front of Egyptian royalty.

My face grew warm and red as I pushed. The room blurred, and I finally gasped in another breath so I didn't pass out.

Whether it was performance anxiety or from skipping lunch, for the life of me, I couldn't produce.

I racked my brain, trying to remember how I'd escaped before.

Crap. I hadn't.

The museum's medical professional had pulled me out somehow. And the other day, Aunt Lucille had slapped me back into the physical realm.

I cupped my hands around my mouth.

"Mom!"

Quiet...

"Dad! Leyla!"

My voice reverberated throughout the empty palace.

Nothing.

Sweat beaded on my forehead.

My aunt wasn't staying with us any longer, but she *was* psychic. Her "gift" had warned her of my predicament. There's no reason it couldn't again.

"Aunt Lucille?" I said, quieter.

I waited.

Please... Call Mom and have her check up on me.

Somebody would find me eventually, right?

My heartbeat quickened. This was the land of the dead.

Nobody heard me.

Nobody was coming.

Relax, I told myself, pacing in front of the throne. Keeping me here was a scare tactic.

That, or a test. He wanted to see whether I could claw my way out of the underworld.

I froze.

Claws.

Aunt Lucille's spirit guide. Well, my spirit guide. I guess.

"Jinx?" I whispered.

Something raked across my face, knocking me onto my hands and knees.

"Ow." I reached up to my temple, and my fingers came back with specks of blood.

Fingers with specks of blood against a backdrop of carpet. I was home, in my room, and in my own clothes.

Jinx sat on the floor before me. She blinked and kicked a card beneath my dresser with her back paw.

"I can't believe that worked."

My spirit guide meowed.

"Thanks." I grabbed the cat and held her to my chest. "You saved my butt."

She purred and nuzzled closer.

Maybe cats weren't so bad.

I held her up and stared into the animal's yellow eyes. "You can't help me break this curse, can you?"

Jinx cocked her head to the side. *Mrr?*

The top of the stairs creaked, and a moment later, Mom appeared in my doorway.

"How's the magic act going?"

I shrugged. "Not great."

"Sorry, honey, but it's bedtime."

"But it's only—" I twisted around and caught the glow of the clock.

Nine p.m. Tut had kidnapped me for three hours.

Mom turned my head and investigated the three tiny scratches. "You're bleeding, honey. What happened?"

"Jinx scratched me. She didn't mean to."

Of course, Leyla picked then to barge into the room.

"Because you're crushing her, twerp," she said, ripping the kitten from my grasp.

"Hey!" Mom jumped between us. "No tug of war with the kitten." She frowned. "We should take her to the vet. Make sure she has all her shots. Maybe have her declawed."

"You can't declaw cats," Leyla said, turning her back and leaving my room. "That's cruel. And illegal in a lot of states."

Mom rolled her eyes. "When did you become an expert on cats?"

"After Aunt Lucille gave me this little cutie," Leyla said from across the hall.

I yawned.

"See, you're tired," Mom said. "Pajamas. Toothbrush. Bed."

"Okay, Mom."

"And wash those scratches so they don't get infected." She pulled me into a hug. "With soap."

Other than my bedtime routine, that was about the last thing I remembered that night. Apparently, getting trapped in a pyramid by a three-thousand-year-old ghost takes a lot out of you.

The next morning began like any other: my annoying alarm clock jolting me out of bed, followed by my parents yelling at me to get up. That led to me picking out clothes, packing my backpack, and finally sitting down at the kitchen table with a bowl of cereal.

Dad limped into the kitchen with his boot and pecked Mom on the cheek.

"Don't forget, I'm having dinner with Pete tonight, so you guys are on your own."

Mom nodded. "Well, some genius scheduled a meeting at five o'clock, so I'm thinking pizza."

Dad came up and ruffled my hair. "Good luck with the talent show."

"Wait, what?" Milk and Cocoa Pebbles dribbled down my chin.

"Gross," Mom said, handing me a napkin.

"The talent show," Dad repeated.

I swallowed and wiped my mouth. "The talent show isn't until Thursday."

Dad blinked. "Today *is* Thursday."

"Real funny, Dad."

He looked at Mom and back at me. "I'm being serious. Today is Thursday. This magic thing must have you super stressed."

I leapt out of my chair, ran to my backpack, and checked the date on the laptop.

Tut had stolen a lot more than three hours.

CHAPTER 12
OUT OF ORDER

My stomach twisted into a jumble of knots from which even Houdini couldn't escape. Two days.

Two.

Whole.

Days.

How did nobody notice I'd been missing?

Why wasn't I starving?

How did I not poop myself?

And the clock kept ticking while I came to grips with my missing time.

The kitchen timer rang.

"John," Mom called out. "You're going to miss the bus."

She rounded the corner, almost running into me. "Oh. There you are. Your cereal's all soggy, but you need to go. Do you want a breakfast bar for the road?"

I shook my head. "I'm not hungry anymore."

She stood there for a moment, then set her steaming coffee cup on the entryway table.

"You haven't been yourself the last two days."

So, I wasn't missing?

"You're nervous about the magic show, huh?"

I nodded. "I'm worried about humiliating myself in front of the whole school. Then the ghost of Harry Houdini will never break King Tut's curse."

Okay, obviously I didn't say any of that. I did nod, though.

"You've been practicing the last three nights straight."

I looked up at her. "I have?"

When Mom raised an eyebrow, I said it again, this time with a healthy dose of faked confidence. "I have."

"You've got this, honey."

"Thanks," I said with a smile. This time I felt it.

Why wouldn't I? Every day, the curse imparted more ancient Egypty facts. Maybe the same was true about magic. All that fancy sleight of hand was nothing but muscle memory. I had this.

"Now get your butt to the bus stop, Mister."

The bus ride consisted of me sitting silently in my seat, searching my brain for the tiniest memory from the last two days.

Jinx smacking me awake was the first thing I remembered after my failed attempts at magic.

I had a sinking feeling even before I started digging around my bag. It confirmed my fears. Even if my entranced doppelganger had learned the routine in the last few days, he hadn't packed the necessities.

My bag contained only school supplies. No playing cards. No empty sports drink bottle. Not even a stray coin.

The bus screeched to a stop and so did any confidence I'd found. I was completely unprepared. All I'd do was make a fool of myself and anger my teacher. And Poodini.

"You have to get off," the driver called.

I looked up and realized I was the last kid on the bus. "Sorry."

I grabbed my bag and raced down the aisle.

Of course that was the perfect time for a stray orange to roll across the floor. It slipped under my right foot, and I landed on my face.

"Sorry," I said through a mouth full of backpack.

As I picked myself up, I noticed a bumblebee crawling beneath the seats.

Ugh. I didn't even grab a bottle of honey from the pantry before I left.

I shuffled into the school and paused in front of the nurse's office.

Going home sick would save me a lot of embarrassment. Technically, Poodini hadn't given a deadline of *when* I had to learn magic.

Hmm... That wasn't quite right. He'd mentioned the talent show. And then there was my best friend...

Other John had volunteered to do this alongside me. He'd never forgive me for letting him do this alone. Plus, if I went home, my friends couldn't help me fill in my missing time.

I turned down the hallway, greeted by loud voices and laughter. A stuffed elephant flew out of our classroom and landed at my feet.

I picked up the stuffie with a smile.

Mrs. Barwick would never allow this level of chaos. She must have been sick. And since she was the talent show lead, they'd postpone it to another day. Right?

Nope. Just a classroom of kids preparing for their five minutes of fame.

Martin stood by the door juggling stuffed animals. Britta bounced up and down on an honest-to-goodness pogo stick. Krista hula-hooped in a tutu, knocking a cup of pens off a nearby desk. Someone at the back of the room played a recorder so off-key I couldn't identify the song.

Meanwhile, Mrs. Barwick sat behind her desk with her nose in a book, ignoring it all. Apparently, the talent show was like a day off for the teachers.

I tossed the elephant in the air. Marty caught it... and dropped the cat and rabbit. Seeing that little stumble raised my spirits.

In fact, nobody seemed particularly good at their craft. Except Krista. But girls naturally had a knack for hula-hooping.

Mrs. Barwick would probably be okay with my lousy act. Hopefully, Poodini would be too.

I caught sight of my friends in their usual seats and headed their way.

This was the first time I'd seen Other John without his multi-pocketed fishing jacket. Instead, he wore one of those tacky tuxedo tee shirts.

Akira and Park had on their typical sports attire. The three of them stopped talking as soon as they caught sight of me.

"Uhh... What's going on, guys?" I said, dropping my bag and sliding into my desk.

"Phew," Other John said. "You're finally back."

I looked between my friends. "I wasn't at school the last two days?"

"Oh, you were here. You just seemed..."

"What?" I leaned closer and whispered, "Possessed?"

"Distracted," Park said.

"Sleepwalky," said Akira at the same time as her brother.

Other John pointed at her. "Ooh. That's more accurate. It was like you were sleepwalking."

"Hold up," Park spoke up again, his eyes going wide. "*Were* you possessed?"

"I don't know." I shrugged my shoulders. "But I remember nothing from the last two days."

"Your body was here, but your brain was elsewhere." Akira said. "You ignored everyone. Except Mrs. Barwick. She called on you for a question, and you just..."

"Stared at her and let out the world's longest fart," Park finished.

Great.

"Guess the scarab didn't work as planned."

"Sorry, guys." I turned to face Other John. "Tut held me hostage so I couldn't learn the magic routine. All I have is stupid jokes."

I hung my head in my hands. "The show will be a disaster. Mrs. Barwick will fail me."

Akira cleared her throat. "It doesn't count toward our grades."

Other John pulled his backpack on his desk and dug through it. "Here," he said, throwing a tuxedo shirt at me. "And don't worry. After you hadn't snapped out of it yesterday, I packed all the props we'll need. Here."

He pulled out a deck of cards, a silver ring, an elastic band, some coins, a glass... Everything on my list.

"You're a genius! I owe you big time."

He smiled. "Enough for you to stop calling me Other John?"

"Nope." Akira and Park said together.

"Any chance you have a container of honey in there too? I still owe King Tut his tribute."

"Yeah," said Other John, reaching back into the bag.

I sat up in my seat. "Really?"

"No." He started loading everything into an empty cardboard box. "Why would I bring honey to school?"

"Oh..."

Akira muttered something about him being less cruel, only for the bell to interrupt her.

Mrs. Barwick slipped a bookmark into her book and set it down.

"Alright, class, please settle down. We still have two hours of work before we gather in the auditorium for the talent show. Ms. Tanner's class volunteered to go first this year. We will have our turn after lunch."

The door opened, and Buttcrack Steve strolled into the classroom.

Mrs. Barwick tapped her foot and waited as the bully took his time settling in the last open desk. His bag hit the floor with a loud, wooden clunk.

"As I was saying," she said, glaring at Buttcrack Steve. "Following lunch, you will each have ten minutes to showcase your talents."

Mrs. Barwick pulled on her bifocals and checked her clipboard.

"Starting with... John Pahrsink and John Shaw."

"You mean 'Other John'," Park whispered.

Akira snickered.

Buttcrack Steve's hand shot up. "Actually, Mrs. Barwick, I'd like to go first if that's okay."

She did a double-take and looked at us. "Any objections, Johns?"

I looked over and hardly recognized my bully.

For once, Steve had combed his hair. He wore a buttoned-down shirt with a collar. Not to mention shorts with a belt, effectively canceling out his nickname.

But he grinned like the same old cartoon shark staring down a helpless minnow.

"None here," Other John said.

"Very well," our teacher continued. "Stephen will go first, followed by the Johns, Krista—"

She assigned the rest of the class their order, reminded everyone to be respectful and so on. At least, I presume that's what she did.

Her words became lost in the shuffle of my mind. Or was it a result of the curse's time-traveling effects? Because, honestly, the rest of the morning, lunch included, passed in an incoherent blur.

I don't remember our short lesson that morning. Or the next hour in the auditorium while Ms. Tanner's students did their thing. The next thing I became aware of was sitting in the first row in front of the stage.

My left arm felt weird... tight. My heart raced.

Were those signs of a heart attack? Nah. I was too young for a heart attack.

But when I looked down, I realized I'd somehow pulled the tuxedo shirt on over my own tee. Other John was just a bit smaller than me.

"I hope you're ready," Other John said. "We're next."

I tried to straighten out the shirt as best I could and looked at him. My best friend had put on a cape and a top hat. Marty sat on the other side of me, a bag of various juggling props snug in his lap.

"I guess so," I whispered as Mrs. Barwick took the stage.

Other John breathed a sigh of relief as our teacher tapped the microphone.

"Next up for my fifth-grade class is Stephen."

Buttcrack Steve marched out and set down a small wooden crate in the middle of the stage.

He hopped onto the stool, pulled a doll with blonde spiky hair from the wooden case, and plopped it on his lap.

The tan paint on its face was worn and cracked but there was no mistaken who it resembled. It had a pair of square glasses drawn on with marker. Plus, it had a "J" and a "P" sloppily drawn on its red shirt.

That's when I noticed the jaw. It wasn't a doll. It was one of those creepy dummies (not that there's any other kind of dummy).

Buttcrack Steve stared me dead in the eye and flashed those shark teeth.

He turned to the shabby prop. "Why don't you introduce yourself to all these people?"

"My name is Juan Fartstink," said the "doll." "And I'm a dummy."

CHAPTER 13
MAGIC FOR... DUMMIES?

It was by far the worst start to a ventriloquist gig I'd ever seen. Buttcrack Steve didn't try to keep his mouth still. Nor did he bother changing the tone of his voice.

The big dummy pinched his nose shut and kicked the wooden crate across the stage. "Now I know why you were locked up in that box," he said in a nasally voice. "You stink."

"Don't blame that on me." The dummy looked my way and gestured with its head. "I think it's someone in the audience."

To his credit, he stopped holding his nose, and his voice went back to normal for his lifeless companion. I take that back. He deserved nothing since the entire routine was to insult me.

"So what do you think of our school, John?"

(That's not a typo. He'd already stopped calling the stupid thing Juan.)

"It stinks."

"And my classmates?"

"They stink, too," the dummy said without its mouth moving. Not that it had matched up with any of the words before.

He wrenched the dummy's head backward with a crack, shoving its nose up its butt.

"Oops. That *is* me. All I do is fart, all day long." Spittle sparkled like glitter under the stage lights as Buttcrack Steve stuck out his tongue and let out an exaggerated fart.

One or two people chuckled. Steve sat up straighter, feeding off their laughter.

He set the dummy on his knee, but its head drooped forward, refusing to stay up.

"You know, John, you're the worst dummy I've ever seen."

"But I'm not a dummy." For the millionth time, he turned that creepy thing's head toward me. "I'm a voodoo doll."

Stephen gasped and flung the broken dummy into the air. Dried flakes of paint rained down as the doll sailed within inches of the ceiling.

It crashed into the ground with a dull thud. Wood splintered as pieces broke off the dummy.

(I'll admit it, I flinched—which gave Buttcrack Steve another laugh).

"Thank you, Stephen," Mrs. Barwick said.

He looked up at the clock. "But my time isn't over."

"You can finish your act for the principal. In his office."

Buttcrack Steve gave a deep bow before sticking his hand in his shirt and farting with his armpit.

Mrs. Barwick growled and showed off her own talent. She scooped up the box with one hand, guided the bully offstage with her other, and pushed the broken dummy along with her foot.

Her heel clipped one of the dummy's stray eyeballs. Naturally, it flew off the stage, bounced a few times, and rolled to a stop at my feet.

She motioned us onstage. We slid out of our seats and made our way up the stairs. Other John dragged a small table to the center.

"Next, John Pahrsink and John Shaw will delight us with some magic."

I looked down at the Post-it note Other John had given me earlier. The first trick was my responsibility.

Unfortunately, I couldn't do anything under the frozen spotlight but worry.

Poodini hadn't shown himself since Monday. Or if he had, I didn't remember because of Tut.

Was my fart ghost still floating around or did I need to pass him again? There. On the stage. In front of every fifth grader in the school...

I pushed. My stomach protested. Not even a little squeaker.

Mrs. Barwick gestured from off-stage.

I cleared my throat and checked the sticky note again. The coin trick. Right.

I hadn't practiced it at all, what could go wrong?

"I have in my hand an empty glass," I said, mimicking the video from the other night.

A few people laughed.

You already look like a buffoon, Poodini said with a sigh. I glanced around. There was no sign of the ghost, just my nervous subconscious taunting me.

My brain redeemed itself because it was Dad's voice that came next.

Interject humor. You've got this.

I grabbed a glass from Other John's box of stuff and held it up.

"Ta-da. Magic!"

That got a couple of honest laughs.

I could do this.

"And an ordinary length of exercise band," I said as I took it from the box.

I stretched the band over the mouth of the glass, careful not to dislodge the quarter already trapped inside.

"And one ordinary coin."

I grabbed a quarter from the box by the edges and showed it to the audience before setting it on top of the band.

"Now... let's get that *change.*"

Someone in the front row groaned at the pun. However, both teachers chuckled. At least it was something.

I placed the quarter in my palm, slapped it against the exercise band, and prayed the tape held.

The quarter clinked into the bottom of the glass.

"Ta-da."

I walked to the edge of the stage. "Any volunteers want to inspect the glass?"

Krista's hula hoop clattered to the floor as she shot out of her seat. "I'll do it."

I knelt, and she took the glass from me.

Meanwhile, I scraped the coin off my palm and into the pocket of my jeans.

"Can you confirm the band is still securely around the glass?"

Krista turned it upside down and gave it a shake. The quarter rattled around safely inside.

"And there are no holes in it?"

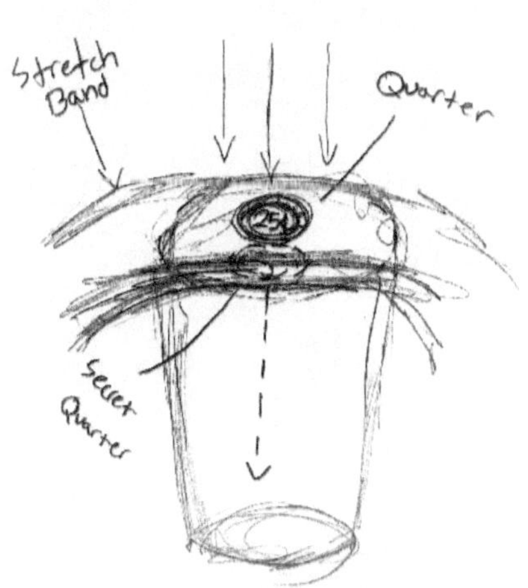

She tugged on the band until it came off and then stretched it in front of her eyes. That wasn't exactly supposed to happen, but the trick was already done. So whatever.

"No," she said, handing the glass back.

"Thank you."

She smiled at me and brushed her hair behind her ear.

Huh. Mom was wrong. Girls *did* like magic.

I scooped the quarter from the glass and handed it to her. "A souvenir for a great assistant," I said with a wink.

Krista hurried back to her seat.

I glanced at Mrs. Barwick to gauge her reaction. Something shifted behind her—a partially see-through man in a top hat.

Great. The first trick had gone off without a hitch. Freedom from the curse was one step closer.

Though as we locked eyes, Poodini put his hand over his mouth in an exaggerated yawn.

He stepped out from behind my teacher and bowed. The hat popped off his head, which he balanced on a single finger.

Other John was too busy getting out the props for the next trick to notice. He slid past me. "You owe me a quarter," he whispered.

"For our next trick—" my partner began.

Poodini thrust his hand inside the hat and pulled forth a cartoonish rabbit. It lifted a paw to its mouth, stifling its own yawn.

I bumped into John and nodded toward my ghost. "Let me do the next one too," I whispered.

My friend backed away.

"John the Magnificent," he said loudly, "will make a bottle disappear before your very eyes."

"One ordinary Gatorade bottle."

I pulled the item from the box and tapped on the cap before placing it carefully on the table.

Let me explain how this trick should have gone. That wasn't an ordinary Gatorade bottle. Other John had carefully removed the label, cut the plastic so only the top and bottom remained, and taped the label back in place.

It wouldn't hold any amount of weight and... Well, you've probably figured out the rest.

I set the bottle down and grabbed the next object. "One plain brown lunch bag."

Poodini caught my eye. He had taken a seat on the stage and started playing a game of cards with the rabbit.

I needed to step up my game.

"Let me show you how I recycle."

I looked over my shoulder. "Throw me the bottle," I whispered.

Other John shook his head.

I nodded, gesturing to my bored ghost.

He shrugged and tossed the bottle.

I stretched open the bag. Then I realized he'd thrown it just out of my reach.

No biggie. We had the entire stage to ourselves. But I presume you know my luck by now.

As I took a step, my foot slid out from under me. The dummy's other eyeball shot into space, and my legs went in opposite directions.

"Owww..."

The bottle hit the ground and the label fell apart, ruining what little illusion remained.

"Have a nice trip," Other John said. "See you next fall."

Several of our classmates laughed. All eyes switched to him like it had been part of the act.

"You okay?" he whispered.

I nodded and then lay flat on my back. The pain in my hamstrings and groin disagreed.

He walked past me and adjusted the mic.

"How were the ancient Egyptians like a fat kid eating beans?"

Other John waited a moment.

"They had a Toot-in-common."

The crowd laughed.

My eyes went wide.

What was he doing? If Toot heard—

One laugh rose above the others, derailing my thought.

Actually, "laugh" wasn't the best description. It was more of an obnoxious, hundred-decibel cackle.

I sat up.

Poodini had been the one laughing. And why wouldn't a grown man enjoy a fart joke? Especially at the expense of the man who'd tried recruiting him as a servant.

Huh.

"Tell another one," I whispered.

"How did King Tutankhamun attract the ladies?" He paused briefly for dramatic effect. "Pharaoh-mones."

More laughter from Poodini. Our teacher chuckled.

"Why did ancient Egyptians measure everything based off the length of the Pharaoh's various body parts?"

I'd heard this one before, so I hopped to my feet and delivered the punchline.

"Because the Pharaoh was their ruler."

That drew some more chuckles from the crowd.

Before either of us could start another, Mrs. Barwick walked across the stage.

"Thank you, boys."

I blinked. That was all we got?

Two tricks (one bungled horribly) and a handful of lame jokes?

Ten minutes in a dentist chair with someone stabbing your gums lasted a lifetime. But when your life was on the line, ten minutes took no time at all.

Other John picked up the box of props and headed off.

I scanned the crowd for Poodini.

He'd pulled a disappearing act again.

Taking with him my dignity and any hope of breaking the curse.

CHAPTER 14
POODINI'S (BRAIN) DUMP

I hung my head and followed Other John through the heavy curtain to the room behind the stage. They wanted us to take the long way around to the back of the auditorium, rather than disrupt the next presenter.

"Next up we have the hula-hoop stylings of Krista," came Mrs. Barwick's voice from the stage.

John paused, cradling the cardboard box against his chest.

"Sorry it didn't go so well," he said, clamping his other hand on my shoulder. "I shouldn't have thrown the bottle."

"Nah. It's my fault. You knew it was a bad idea." I sighed. "Poodini thought the act was lame anyway. I should have known I didn't stand a chance."

"So now what?"

I shrugged. "My aunt suggested breaking into a petting zoo."

"Count me in. I love a good heist movie. We can easily cram a kid into your backpack." The box started slipping from his grasp, and he set it down on a nearby stool. "A baby goat, not like, a child."

"I know baby goats are called kids."

"Okay," Other John said. "Just making sure you didn't think I was a weirdo."

He scratched his nose. "But we don't have to like... hurt the goat, do we?"

"I don't know."

"Wait," he said, his eyes lighting up. "I got it. There's this farming charity that sends out catalogs every Christmas. You can donate livestock to under-privileged countries. Why not ship goats straight to the museum?"

He laughed. "Seriously. Imagine their faces if a delivery guy came in with a dozen goats?"

A shiver ran down my spine and fog clouded my glasses.

Other John must have felt the temperature change too, because he spun at the same time I did. His hands slapped his shirt, forgetting he'd traded the fishing vest for the fake tuxedo.

"Uh, John..."

"Relax," I said. A lump grew in my throat. "He only wants me."

Hopefully.

Poodini whooshed through the air and hovered in front of me.

"That was the worst display of illusion I've ever seen in my life... And afterlife, mind you."

I threw up my hands. "Tut cheated. He kidnapped me and I had no time to practice."

"Yes," Poodini said with a click of his tongue. "Tut..."

That was a tone I'd heard from my parents many times. He knew.

The specter came within inches of my face.

"You are *not* giving me over to King Tutankhamun. I will not serve as his vizier."

I clamped my eyes shut. This was it. Poodini was about to turn me into a rabbit.

"But you're a ghost," he mocked. "What else do you have to do? You'll find out after you die, John. But that won't be today."

"What?" I opened my eyes again.

The ghost backed away. He ran his fingers through his slicked back hair (not that it moved a bit).

"I'll still assist you with all I've learned about your curse."

"You will?"

Poodini nodded. "You need help. Desperately. I'm a man of my word."

His hands came to rest on his hips. "But first, I have a question for you. Will you continue practicing your sleight of hand?"

My first instinct was to lie, but I figured it unwise to add more promises I couldn't keep. I licked my lips. "No. I don't think it's for me."

"Phew," he said, wiping his brow. "You can say that again."

It was the truth, but for some reason that stung.

"And you..." he said, turning to Other John. "I wouldn't quit your day job either."

"I'm eleven, dude. I don't *have* a day job."

But Poodini had already moved on, rubbing his hands together. "Where to begin?

"Okay. First things, first. Curses aren't real and neither is magic."

Other John raised a finger. "But—"

"Don't interrupt."

My buddy twisted his fingers in front of his mouth and threw away a pretend key.

Poodini cringed. "And don't do that either. Mimes are creepy, even to us ghosts."

He looked back at me. "What I was trying to say is that curses and magic aren't real *for the living*. You will never command the power to break Tut's curse."

The ghost got up in Other John's face. "And before you ask, he's got a couple thousand years of experience on me, and he holds the book of the dead. I can't break his curse either."

My stomach sank.

"However, I *can* outsmart him."

Other John and I looked at each other and back at Poodini.

"Let me guess," the ghost continued. "When he first took you to his pyramid, it was completely empty."

I nodded.

"Neither of you look like you're rich."

"Dude, we're e-lev-en," Other John said.

"So you couldn't have afforded that golden receptacle full of saffron."

Wait... He was right. We couldn't, but it was there all the same.

"What *did* you give him?" Poodini asked.

"Just a few strands in an envelope," I said. "From my friend Akira."

Poodini spread his arms out. "You didn't give him a few strands."

"Yeah he—" Other John started. He shut his mouth when Poodini stared.

"No. You delivered a symbolic gesture loaded with intent."

My friend and I stared at one another.

The fart ghost shook his head in his hand.

"I'll explain it like you're five. It's like all the terrible crayon drawings you used to give your mom. She loved them and hung them on the refrigerator even though they looked like garbage scribbles. Your offerings aren't as important as the intent they're based upon. Use that to your advantage.

"Well, best of luck," he said, floating through the wall of the auditorium.

"Wait," I said, but warmth had already begun returning to the room.

There was a ghostly sigh, and Poodini's head stuck out of a little emergency exit sign.

"What?"

"I get it. And thank you. But how do I deliver things to him? I can't bring armloads of stuff to the museum every time he asks for something."

"Are you asking for directions to Duat?"

Other John looked at me.

"It's the Egyptian version of the underworld," I whispered.

"One can only enter Duat via the deceased's tomb. As I said..."

Poodini's last words echoed backstage as he faded from view. "Best of luck."

"So the great goat heist includes a road trip to Egypt?" Other John said.

Yeah... like that was possible.

Footsteps echoed on the stage. Both John and I grabbed for the box before Mrs. Barwick caught us.

A hula hoop rolled along the floor and fell against the wall. Krista chased after it and stopped, eyes darting between the two of us.

"John was watching from backstage," my friend blurted out. "But not in a creepy way."

Krista's mouth went slack, then slowly turned up into a smile.

"Really? What trick was your favorite?"

"Uhh..." I stammered.

Other John elbowed me in the ribs.

"When you spun around and flipped the hoop?"

She flashed another smile.

"Thanks. I'm glad you liked it. You should get back before someone notices you're gone."

I let John take the box and waved her ahead. "After you."

Other John and I walked as slowly as possible, so our conversation remained private.

"I'm sorry a famous magician didn't have the power to break your curse," said Other John. "But at least he gave you something helpful. Right?"

That he had.

My brain had already begun cooking up plans for speeding along my service to the Pharoah. It all began with dinner...

When I got home, Mom was in her office on a conference call. Like usual, Leyla wasn't home from school yet. The coast was clear.

I set my backpack in front of the pantry and started shopping.

Behind some cans of beans, I found an almost full plastic bear of honey. We only had one, but if Poodini's logic held true, it was plenty.

A can of soup fell over as I tossed the honey in my bag. Did Egyptians eat cream of celery? Probably not. I stood it back up and continued my hunt.

Fruit salad in light syrup? Why wouldn't kings eat fruit? One of the little plastic bubbles went into the bag.

Granola bar. Surely, the Egyptians ate oats, right? And raisins sucked, so he got a double dose of that.

Tortillas?

No. Tacos were delicious but didn't culturally fit.

After some thought, I reconsidered my stance on Tea. It was super valuable back in the day.

I stole a bag of each flavor from the variety pack: chamomile, black, green, sleepy time.

Hmm... Anything else?

Cool Ranch Doritos might blow King Tut's mind, but not necessarily in the right way.

Maybe canned tuna? Egyptians lived along the Nile. Fish must have been a big part of everyone's diet. The can slapped against my laptop as I dropped it in.

I took inventory of the bag. Grains. Fruit. Spices. Meat. Sugar. That covered all the main food groups except for dairy.

I walked to the refrigerator and opened the drawer. A little red cylinder of cheese drew my eye. Babybel was only fitting. After all, the cheese I used to love had caused this whole mess.

That covered everything except for the goat.

But I had a plan for that as well.

As I zipped my backpack, the door to Mom's office opened.

"I thought I heard you digging around in the pantry," she said.

I smiled. "Just looking for a snack."

"Do you have any homework?"

I shook my head. "The talent show took most of the day."

"Oh right. How did your magic act turn out?"

"Not so great, but it turned out okay in the end."

"Good." Mom gave me a quick hug. "Don't eat too much junk food. Pizza tonight, remember?"

"We had pizza at school today. Could we try gyros instead?"

"I didn't know you liked gyros. Yeah, I guess we can do that. I have another hour or so of work, then I'll pick something up. You're good until then?"

"Yup."

While Mom went back to work, I enacted phase two of my plan.

I snatched up an old dish rag nobody would miss.

I cut a two-inch strip from one of Dad's adjustable belts.

I trimmed some fringe off one of Mom's scarves.

Cotton. Leather. Wool. That covered all the main textiles.

My scavenger hunt took me to every room in the house, pocketing treasures of all sorts.

The quartz crystal from my aunt.

A silver ring out of Leyla's jewelry box (Don't judge. It didn't even fit my finger, so it wouldn't fit hers. She wouldn't notice it missing.)

And finally, a sheet of gold foil from Mom's untouched scrapbooking supplies.

Precious gems. Silver. Gold.

Check, check, and check. What else could a king want?

A door slammed on the other side of the house.

"Dinner!" Mom yelled.

I dropped my backpack by my bed and raced down the stairs.

She watched as I slid into a chair.

"I only had to call once. You must be hungry."

I nodded as she dished out the food. Everyone got a piece of flatbread loaded with thinly sliced meat, onions, and a cream sauce. A family-sized basket of French fries sat in the center of the table.

"Gyros aren't your usual go-to. Why the sudden interest?"

"I don't know," I said with a shrug. "I guess I was curious how goat tasted."

Leyla stepped up to the table in time to ruin my night.

"Gyro meat isn't goat, you idiot. It's beef and lamb."

CHAPTER 15
IMPROPER OFFERINGS

"Leyla! Apologize to your brother," Mom said.

My sister mumbled something resembling an apology. But I cared more about my mix-up than anything else.

"This isn't goat?" I asked.

Mom glared at Leyla briefly before answering. "No. It's a mixture of meats, but usually not goat. Gyros mean 'to turn' in Greek. The food's named that way because the meat is spit-roasted."

Mom trailed off and stared into the distance for a moment before shaking her head. "I've been married to your father for too long. I'm starting to sound like him."

Leyla pushed her plate away from her. "Eww... I'm not eating spit."

I laughed. "A spit is a skewer used to slowly turn meat for roasting. Who's the idiot now?"

Mom glared at me. "That goes for you too. Be nice. You're the only siblings each other will ever have."

"Thank God," we said under our breaths together.

Mom laughed. "Aunt Lucille and I probably sounded like that when we were your age."

Leyla took a French fry, dipped it into the sauce, and tasted it. "Pretty good."

I picked strips of onion out of my sandwich and planned a way out of this one. Goats and sheep weren't all *that* different. They were roughly the same size. People made clothing from their wool, and cheese from their milk.

Tut was just a teen when he died. Maybe he wouldn't know the difference either.

"Can you pass me a napkin?"

Mom passed one over. Grease soaked through the napkin as I tucked two large strips of mystery meat inside and stuffed it in my pocket.

I ate the rest. And more than my fair share of fries. Tut wasn't getting any of those. There were no deep fryers three thousand years ago. Besides, they were too good to waste.

"I'm going to go upstairs and work on my homework," I said as I brought my plate to the dishwasher.

Mom's chair scratched against the floor as she shifted to look at me. "You told me earlier that you didn't have any homework."

Oops. She was right.

"It's not due till next week. I wanted to get a head start so I don't have to work on it over the weekend."

Her eyes narrowed, checking my face for signs of a lie.

"I'm going up to my room too," Leyla said, leaving her seat. "Janey is supposed to call."

Mom pointed at me. "First, you're loading the dishwasher." She directed her finger at my sister. "Your job is putting away the leftovers and washing the table."

While Leyla groaned, I collected the rest of the plates and tossed the garbage.

Mom curled up on the couch with her phone, and I headed upstairs.

Once my sister's door clicked shut, I got to work.

Visiting the museum this late was out of the question. And I couldn't enter Duat since Tut's tomb was in Egypt.

"Toot?" I called out. "Are you there?"

Crickets.

Well, not exactly. If I listened carefully, I could make out Leyla gossiping across the hall.

No ghosts floated through the wall. Likewise, my ~~stomach~~ butt didn't make a peep. Strangely, that large, greasy meal hadn't produced any gas.

Time for plan C.

With backpack in hand, I locked myself in the bathroom and started lining the counter with my offerings. The scent of gyros lingered in the air. And my hands. And my shorts. I'd hear about that on laundry day.

I stood in front of the toilet, legs shoulder-width apart and raised the bottle of honey in one hand and the goat in the other.

Intent, I reminded myself.

I cleared my throat.

"King Tutankhamun, I return that which was taken from you. Please accept these humble offerings and be made whole."

Toilet water splashed up at me as the meat—which looked surprisingly like you-know-what—dropped into the bowl. A thick coil of honey poured from the little plastic bear until my hands couldn't squeeze any longer.

The bottle gasped for air as I let go, letting out a loud "fart"' I laughed but quickly composed myself again. This was serious business.

The plastic bear farted again as I strangled it to death.

"Eww..." came Leyla's voice from the hall. "My little brother's laughing while destroying our toilet. Boys are so gross."

Embarrassing, but I couldn't stop now. I farted out the rest of the bear's insides and pressed the lever on the tank.

Water whisked the honey and beef (or chicken?) to Duat. Air gurgled through the pipes, sounding suspiciously like, "Accepted."

Like a deranged chef, I fed the toilet its second course: the mini wheel of cheese, chunky all-white tuna, bite-sized pieces of granola bars, and tea-leaf potpourri.

My greasy gyro-fingers struggled opening the fruit cup.

"Come on..."

The plastic bubble slipped from my grasp, splashing toilet water and tiny flakes of tea all over my face.

Ugh.

After washing my face half a dozen times, I returned to the toilet.

Bits of tuna were already breaking apart, while granola floaters bobbed up and down among the tea leaves on the water's surface. Somewhere beneath all that was an entire fruit cup.

Hopefully Poodini was right because my sickly gray soup of the day didn't look fit for a king.

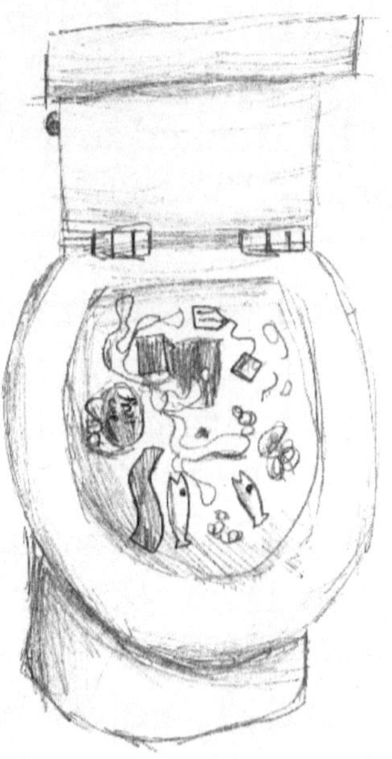

I covered my hand with tissues and flushed, waiting to grab the cup after everything went down the pipes.

The toilet hadn't lost its appetite.

Specks of tea leaves floated back up, but it swallowed everything else. Plastic fruit cup and all.

With a shrug, I moved on.

I tossed in the wool scraps and the strip of leather from Dad's belt. The dish rag worried me, so I tore it into bite-sized strips.

After it flushed, I moved onto dessert.

The geode, ring, and gold foil flushed without a hitch.

I wiped my hands together and realized something. I'd served Tut a grand buffet, but nothing to drink. Unless the fruit syrup counted. And toilet water tea.

Oh well. It wasn't like I could have stolen a bottle of wine without anyone noticing. Besides, if this worked out, there would be plenty of other opportunities. I grabbed my bag and opened the bathroom door.

Leyla stared at me from the first step of the stairs. She'd been sitting there this entire time.

"Eww..." she said into the phone. "He didn't even wash his hands."

She ducked around me and slammed her bedroom door.

I sat on the edge of my bed, lifted one cheek, and pushed. Still nothing.

The curse only worked on its own schedule. I was stuck waiting to find out whether Tut received my tribute. Unless...

My spirit guide had rescued me after Tut imprisoned me in Duat. Maybe she could get me back in without going to Egypt.

"Jinx?" I said, sticking my head in the hallway.

Leyla's voice came through the walls loud and clear, but that was all. The cat had to be inside her room. Then I noticed something. A faint scratching at my sister's door with every lull in her side of the conversation.

I crept across the hallway and placed my ear to the wood.

"But are there any cute boys—"

I turned the knob as gently as possible and opened it just a crack.

Jinx slipped between my legs and ducked into my room.

"Oh no, you didn't," Leyla screeched.

I froze, ready for my sister to attack. A giggle followed, and she went back to talking with her friend.

With a sigh of relief, I pulled the door shut.

Jinx waited patiently at my bedside, her tail swishing back and forth.

I sat down next to her.

"Can you get me into Duat?"

Jinx turned her head and stared.

"The Egyptian underworld."

Mrow?

The cat yawned and lowered herself to the bed and shut her eyes.

I sighed. "Fat load of help you are."

She peeked at me with one eye.

"Oh..." I said, smacking my forehead. "I get it. You're telling me to go to sleep."

Jinx leapt off my bed and darted somewhere else in the house.

I glanced at the clock. Seven thirty. Going to bed now would only bring tossing and turning but it was the only way.

And I was right. I lay there overthinking how I could have done things better.

Sourdough. Why hadn't I given Tut sourdough? Lots of care went into making that bread. Oatmeal was mush. And it had a stupid mascot with boring clothes.

Speaking of clothes, Mom constantly pulled clothes out of our closets we'd outgrown. Tut could have used some new threads.

Egypt was hot and the floors in Tut's stone pyramid were rough. Picturing the Pharoah on his throne with his bare feet made me uncomfortable.

I should have sent him sandals. The toilet sucked up that fruit cup, but a pair of sandals? Nah. Better to stick with easily flushable items.

Did they eat rice in ancient Egypt? Or beans? Those were easily flushable. Plus, beans and farts belonged together. Was that a positive or a negative?

What about—

A shadow darted against the wall.

I hadn't remembered farting.

I shot up and caught sight of an all-black figure with the head of a jackal at the foot of my bed.

My heart skipped a beat. That was no fart ghost.

CHAPTER 16
ANUBIS & THE MONO-COLOR DREAM COAT

The jackal-man thing stepped closer, its head brushing against my ceiling. The thing was hairier than Dad, covered in thick black fur. Unlike my dad, rippling muscles covered its torso.

I would have rolled out of bed and run had my legs responded. My arms wouldn't shield my face either as he leaned over the bed, his muzzle inching near my face.

"Wha—What do you want?"

Weird. Nothing else worked but I still had my voice.

I opened my mouth to scream. For my parents. Or Jinx. Or anyone, really.

Meow.

My eyes shifted to the doorway.

Jinx was there with me. She didn't seem the least bit scared of the weird hybrid creature.

Anubis. A voice said in my head. *My voice.*

More inexplicable things about ancient Egypt flooded my brain.

This was no ordinary animal. He was Anubis. The God of the afterlife.

The protecter of lost souls.

The guide to the underworld.

Jinx meowed again from the doorway, her tail twitching rhythmically behind her.

Anubis turned his head.

My spirit guide and the Egyptian god held a staring contest. Minutes later, Jinx emerged victorious.

Anubis faced me again, yellow eyes glowing, his hot doggy breath fogging my glasses.

The Egyptian god extended a single claw-tipped finger, pressed it against my forehead...

And pushed.

My body tumbled through my bed like a bottomless pit. Anubis and Jinx peered down from above, growing smaller with each passing second. Streaks of blue and white from my comforter flew past like shooting stars.

Before my two guides completely faded from view I jerked to a halt and hit the cold, hard floor in Tut's domain.

"Ushabti!" The entire palace shook under the Pharaoh's booming voice.

I jumped to my feet and held my breath as he learned forward on his throne.

"You dare to show yourself here, without my vizier?"

"I'm sorry," I said, fumbling with my hands. "He pulled a disappearing act."

Without taking his eyes off mine, he gestured around the room. "And you thought these offerings would make up for your shortcoming?"

"Yes," I snapped. "No."

"No?"

"I... I'm simply fulfilling my duty."

"These offerings are..." Tutankhamun reclined again. "Acceptable."

Phew.

"Is there anything else I can get you?"

Tutankhamun shook his head and gave a casual wave of his hand.

"These will suffice for now."

I stepped away from the throne. My extra credit paid off. Gleaming bowls containing grains, raisins, and fruit had been spread around the table. Giant silver platters held enormous hunks of steaming meat and whole fish.

It wasn't just the table. Tanned hides and brightly colored rolls of fabric hung over racks and lay on shelves. Elaborate chests overflowing with jewels, gold, and silver sat in one corner of the room.

Poodini had been right. Everything I'd flushed appeared in abundance. For the first time I felt like I'd truly accomplished something.

Except...

I looked from one corner to the next. And then turned around and checked behind me.

I didn't need to count stone bricks to realize the palace had doubled in size since my last visit. And the "banquet" table? It held enough food for an army. Yet, there was as much empty space as when it only held the spice jar.

I faced the throne again.

"What about the curse?" I said.

The corner of his mouth turned up in a smile. "The curse will lift once you've returned *all* my belongings."

My heart sank. He'd never had any intention of releasing me.

I could give Tut everything he asked for until eternity and it wouldn't matter. I tried to focus on the bright side. The Pharoah clearly didn't know gyros were beef either. And he seemed happy. For now.

Plus, I'd learned a lot.

Firstly, the Egyptian god of the underworld had my back. At least, I felt I qualified as a lost soul at this point. That meant it was Anubis' job to guide me (I'm still embarrassed that Jinx beat me to that conclusion.)

Then there was Poodini.

The illusionist had provided a shortcut for fulfilling Tut's ridiculous requests. And it had worked.

More importantly, there were smarter historical figures out there.

Albert Einstein.

Stephen Hawking.

Heck, there had to be a smarty pants who'd love serving as Tut's vizier.

Howard Carter! The archaeologist who'd discovered Tutankhamun's tomb.

I was in grade school. A nobody. If I delivered a more capable replacement, Tut might actually remove the curse.

Before any other bright ideas struck, the pyramid rumbled. By now I knew what that meant.

I'd be awake shortly. And, judging by the violent pains forming in my stomach, farting out a new ghost.

I shot out of bed and rushed to the bathroom like an Olympic runner.

Something unholy gurgled. Only, the sound came from ahead of me.

When I turned the corner, I found Dad with his sleeves rolled up, furiously ramming a plunger into the toilet.

My stomach twisted itself into knots.

Dad looked up, and the sloshing water stopped. "John? Everything okay?"

"I need the bathroom."

The toilet gurgled a duet alongside my stomach.

"You'll have to go downstairs. Mom's in the shower and someone clogged this one."

I clenched my butt and waddled down the stairway. This ghost wasn't like the others. Something enormous wanted out.

I gripped the bottom of the railing, sling-shotting myself around the corner into the dark. Pausing long enough to flip on the light switch would cause an out-of-body experience if you know what I mean.

A white-hot bolt of pain shot up my tail pipe and with it the realization that I wasn't going to make it.

I rounded the final corner, guided by the faint light of traffic passing outside the window.

Home stretch. You've got this.

The lights came on in the bathroom, anticipating my urgent need.

No, not lights. Lightning.

Angry, red forks that foretold doom.

As I crossed the threshold, thunder shook the entire house, and with it my concentration.

A deafening crack rang out, draining the air from my colon and lungs alike.

The fart lifted me from my feet, launching me headfirst into the wall.

Stars blurred my vision.

I gasped for breath and instantly regretted it.

Was that fresh horse manure mixed with microwaved year-old Brussels sprouts?

I touched my head and the back of my pants.

Neither had a lump.

Lightning flashed again, illuminating the snow-white, flowing hair, and long beard of a figure in the doorway.

What the heck did I eat that made me fart out Santa?

More lightning gave me a better glimpse of the visitor.

Santa had ditched his red suit for a bedsheet draped over one shoulder. And his bowl full of jelly? Traded up for a six pack and a leafy crown.

Electricity sparkled in his eyes for a split second before thunder rattled the window.

My jaw hit the floor.

Not Santa. Zeus.

My butt had just birthed the muscle-bound god of thunder.

AFTERWORD
THE END?

Personally, I thought fighting a curse with escape artist magic was brilliant. Someone suggested I should have gone with Harry Potter instead of Harry Houdini but he did get my butt out of a jam.

What do you think? Will a literal god have the power to break the curse?

That is a tale for another day. One I hope you'll return to enjoy.

If you have fan art to share, suggestions on beating the curse, or historic figures you'd like to see, feel free to share! You can reach John at farts@derelictbooks.com.

About the Author

Michael may be an adult, but only on the outside. He still finds fart humor funny and loves video games.

You can follow Michael via these outlets:
    www.derelictbooks.com
    Facebook: @DerelictBooks
    Instagram: @MJAAuthor

Stay up to date by joining his newsletter: